Yukka, Yukka.

"Hand your homework assignments up to the front," said Mr. Matous.

My classmates were smirking. I could tell they were just waiting for what I would do next. I wouldn't disappoint them. I always come up with something.

One by one, my classmates gave their homework to Mr. Matous—everyone except me.

"Bobby," said Mr. Matous. "Did you do your homework?"

"No," I admitted. "I did some other kid's homework."

My Life as a Fifth-Grade Comedian

Elizabeth Levy

HarperTrophy®
A Division of HarperCollinsPublishers

To Murray,
whose loving teaches me how to love
and who always laughs with me

My Life as a Fifth-Grade Comedian
Copyright © 1997 by Elizabeth Levy
For information address HarperCollins Children's Books, a division of
HarperCollins Publishers, 10 East 53rd Street, New York, NY 10022.
Library of Congress Cataloging-in-Publication Data
Levy, Elizabeth.
My life as a fifth-grade comedian / by Elizabeth Levy.
p.   cm.
Summary: Although Bobby's father thinks that he might be expelled just like his
older brother, with the encouragement of a new fifth-grade teacher, Bobby tries to
channel his penchant for humor into a learning experience.
ISBN 0-06-026602-3. — ISBN 0-06-440723-3 (pbk.)
[1. Schools—Fiction.   2. Jokes—Fiction.   3. Fathers and sons—Fiction.
4. Self-perception—Fiction.]   I. Title.
PZ7.L5827Gr   1997   97-3842
[Fic]—DC21   CIP
                                                                        AC
Typography by Al Cetta
First Harper Trophy edition, 1998
❖
Visit us on the World Wide Web!
http://www.harperchildrens.com
12 13 LP/BR 20

Also by Elizabeth Levy

Keep Ms. Sugarman in the Fourth Grade

Cleo and the Coyote

Brian and Pea Brain Mysteries

Rude Rowdy Rumors

A Mammoth Mix-Up

School Spirit Sabotage

Sam and Robert Bamford Books

Dracula Is a Pain in the Neck

Wolfman Sam

Frankenstein Moved in on the Fourth Floor

The Zombies of Central Park

SPECIAL THANKS

To Elva Matous—number-one fan—her great laugh convinced me that I had to write about laughing in schools. To Bonnie Anderson, who believed in Bobby—for her love, friendship and wonderful judgment. To Emilyn Garrick, teacher and friend, whose huge heart is a lesson in what's right with our schools.

To all the kids at P.S. 11, whose writing proves that kids have an unlimited supply of imagination and jokes, and particular thanks to Josh Cain for permission to use his poem "Ode to Road Kill." Also special thanks to Bobby Russell, whose story "Bobby, Mrs. Garrick and the Dangerous Octopus" still makes me laugh.

To Robie Harris, loving friend, cousin and wonderful reader. To Erica Levy, Ben Harris and David Harris, three wonderful newcomers to the teaching profession, who prove that great heart and humor will be in our classrooms well into the twenty-first century.

To my editors—Nancy Siscoe, who poured her heart and mind into this book, and Cylin Busby and Ginee Seo, who shepherded this book home. To Elaine Markson, who believed in this book and fought for it. Finally, to all the wonderful kids and teachers all over the country and the world who wrote or e-mailed me their jokes.

☺

CHAPTER 1

Why was Christopher Columbus a crook?

Because he double-crossed the Atlantic.

"Yuck!" shouted Mr. Matous. The doorknob rattled as he tried to turn it. The class cracked up. They say that laughter is the best medicine. If that's so, then call me the doctor. I was the one who had put Vaseline on the outside doorknob. My brother, Jimmy, taught me that Vaseline was a practical joker's best friend. I don't even want to tell you what Jimmy taught me about Vaseline and a toilet seat.

"Mrs. Harris, could you get me a paper towel? Quickly!" We could hear Mr. Matous yelling to the other fifth-grade teacher from outside the door.

"What did you do?" Janeen asked. Janeen is my best friend. She looked worried. But that wasn't unusual for her.

"Relax," I said. "He'll never be able to prove it was me. Vaseline tells no tales."

"Bobby!" shouted Mr. Matous, still on the other side of the door.

Janeen giggled. "Can't prove it was you, huh? Who else would it be? Yesterday you put green food dye in the science experiment. I think he'll have a clue."

Mr. Matous came into the classroom, wiping his hand. "Bobby," he said, shaking his head.

"Me? What did I do?" I put on my most innocent face. My brother, Jimmy, taught me another thing: Never confess. If you don't confess, adults will always wonder if maybe they're wrong. Of course, this tactic didn't help when they kicked Jimmy out of high school. He was running a gambling ring—real gambling, not just penny poker. He used the high school computers to set up his very own Web page so that customers could place bets. Adults aren't concerned with your not confessing when they have proof of your guilt.

Janeen raised her hand and tried to defend me. "Mr. Matous, it didn't have to be Bobby. There weren't fingerprints on the Vaseline or anything."

Mr. Matous threw the paper towel into the wastepaper basket. "Janeen, there's such a thing as circumstantial evidence. Anyhow, Bobby, let's try for a clean slate—or at least a clean door-knob."

Mr. Matous can be pretty funny. He *likes* to laugh. Some teachers don't, but when you get one who does, you're golden. It's Mr. Matous's first year of teaching. He's the kind of teacher who thinks all kids are worth saving. Everybody in the class knows that I am the type of kid who is too much for Mr. Matous to handle. It's made for an interesting year.

"Hand your homework assignments up to the front," said Mr. Matous. My classmates were smirking. I could tell they were just waiting for what I would do next. I wouldn't disappoint them. I always come up with something. One by one, my classmates gave their homework to Mr. Matous—everyone except me. "Bobby," said Mr. Matous. He sounded tired. "Did you do your homework?"

"No," I admitted. "I did some other kid's homework."

The class tittered. "Bobby, that joke is so old, it has mold on it," said Mr. Matous.

The class laughed hysterically. That's what I love about Mr. Matous. He's as funny as I am. "Quiet!" he shouted. "It wasn't that funny. Bobby, this is the third time in a row that you haven't done your homework. What's the problem?"

"It's not a good time in my life for homework right now." The class cracked up again.

"Now what exactly does that mean?" asked Mr. Matous.

"I mean, there's a lot going on at home right now. I don't have time for homework."

Mr. Matous looked confused. I tend to have that effect on teachers. "Class, open your history books and review the chapter on Columbus's first encounters with Native Americans," he said. He came down the aisle and stood in front of my desk with a concerned look on his face. "What's happening at home that's keeping you from doing your homework?" he asked softly. "If there's really a problem, you know that you can come to me."

I thought about it. First-year teachers are such suckers for hard-luck stories. I could tell him about Jimmy's fight with my parents after he got kicked out of school. I looked out the window. It was a cold March day. I was supposed to meet Jimmy after school. Jimmy's almost eighteen—eight years older than me. He's staying with a friend. I miss him. Home is not exactly a barrel of laughs without Jimmy. He left home, and my parents won't ask him back. They call it tough love, but it seems like tough luck to me. I can just imagine what will happen to me when I step out of line. The wind was blowing. A gust of wind hit a piece of newspaper and sent it tumbling up into the air—as if the laws of gravity had been turned upside down.

"What problems?" repeated Mr. Matous.

"Uh, seriously, Mr. Matous," I said in a loud voice so the other kids could hear, "I would have done my homework, but there was a problem in my house. They cut off the gravity. Dad forgot to pay the bill. He's very absentminded."

I could hear some of my classmates giggling. It was a sound I loved.

"Cut off the gravity," repeated Mr. Matous. Most adults would ask, "Is that supposed to be a joke?" Not Mr. Matous. He was having a hard time keeping a straight face.

"Yeah, things are pretty up in the air right now." I love it when jokes come to me. I'd have to add this one to my notebook. I write down the best jokes that I've heard or made up. I've got a whole shelf full of books on how to be a comic, and they all say the same thing—keep a notebook with you at all times to jot down ideas. But this idea was more than just a joke. I wished something like that could really happen—gravity cutting off. All my problems would float up and away. Unfortunately, Mr. Matous had just about had it with my sense of humor.

"Bobby," said Mr. Matous, "if your homework is late one more time, your parents will come in and talk to the principal. Consider this fair warning."

He walked up to the front of the class. My friend Willie gave me a thumbs-up sign. I knew Willie liked the way I had kept the jokes coming.

"Okay, class," said Mr. Matous, "back to history. The topic under discussion is: Christopher Columbus—a hero or a villain? Two contradictory facts: He was a brilliant navigator and a courageous explorer, but he also exploited the Taino, the natives that he found in the West Indies. I want to hear your opinions, but remember, I want those opinions to be backed up by facts."

Tyrone raised his hand. "I think Columbus was a villain because when he met the Taino, the very first things he thought were about making them servants and about gold."

"But King Ferdinand and Queen Isabella sent him for gold," said Willie. "You can't blame Columbus. He knew he would be considered a failure if he didn't find gold."

I shuffled through my book. I hadn't done the assignment. I felt Janeen nudge me. Mr. Matous must have asked me a question. "Bobby," he repeated, "what's your opinion?"

"About what?" I asked.

"About Columbus," said Mr. Matous. He had that patient sound in his voice that teachers get when they're about to explode.

"I think he was a crook," I said.

"Okay, Bobby," said Mr. Matous. "That's a very legitimate point of view. Do you think Columbus was a crook because he stole gold from the Taino?"

"No," I said. "Columbus was a crook because he double-crossed the Atlantic. He went back and forth three times. What a double-crosser! Triple-crosser! He deserved to be hanged." Sometimes I just love my mind. I may have no memory for history or dates, but I can remember almost any joke I've ever heard.

The class snickered. I could see a little smile on Mr. Matous's lips. But then the smile left his face. "Bobby, do you really think that you can get away with this all year?" he asked.

"Naw, I only got hired for six months." I tried to keep a straight face.

"Six months?" asked Mr. Matous. "What do you mean, hired?"

"The Board of Ed hired me. I'm actually a midget. They send me around to all new teachers to see who can cut it in New York City." The kids around me laughed—everybody except Janeen.

I studied Mr. Matous's face. Had I gone too far? When I start making the people around me laugh, I don't want to stop. It's the soaringest feeling. Even when I know it will get me in trouble, I can't stop.

"All right, class, thanks to Bobby's outburst, we're going to end this discussion. Instead, we'll have a quiz. Please put away your books, and write your name at the top of a piece of paper."

A surprise quiz. I was going to flunk. I didn't know anything about Columbus. I threw my pencil in the air "Oh, no, you want us to remember *our* names. Talk about trick questions!" The class started laughing again.

"Bobby," snapped Mr. Matous, "enough is enough. It's not good for you, and it's not good for me to let you get away with this."

The last thing I needed was another note from school saying that I was in trouble. My father would go ballistic. "I'm sorry, Mr. Matous," I added quickly. "I was out of line."

"Yes, you were," said Mr. Matous. "And you'll go to the principal's office and try to explain to her why you didn't do your homework. Go!"

I got up. Willie was giggling, but Janeen

looked concerned. I hated the idea of Mr. Matous being genuinely angry at me. I also despise going to the principal's office. Sometimes it seems like I spend more time there than I do in class.

CHAPTER 2

Knock, knock.
Who's there?
Cargo.
Cargo Who?
Car go "Beep, beep."

Ms. Lofti, the school secretary, wasn't surprised to see me. "What did you do this time?" she asked. I looked longingly at the jar of cookies that she always keeps on her desk.

"Nothing," I said. "The teacher yelled at me for something I *didn't* do. My homework."

"Yeah, yeah. Have a cookie, Bobby. You told me that joke last week." I felt bad that I was repeating myself.

Dr. Deal came out of her office. I'm scared of Dr. Deal. She doesn't have a sense of humor, but she thinks she does. The worst adults are the ones who think they're funny but aren't. "What are you here for this time, Bobby?" she asked.

"Uh, Mr. Matous wanted me to explain to you why I didn't do my homework."

"Again? What is it with you, Bobby? Do you think there is something special about you that means you don't have to do the assigned work?" Dr. Deal asked.

Why do adults ask this kind of question? Whatever you answer, you're in trouble. "I don't think I'm special," I muttered. At least that was the truth.

"Right now I want you to write Mr. Matous an essay explaining exactly why you didn't do your homework. Make it coherent. Do you understand the word 'coherent'? It means observing logical order and showing intelligence."

"Yes, ma'am," I said, but I felt like asking, "Do you understand the word 'sarcastic'?" She sounded so much like my dad. I instantly got a stomachache. I don't like writing anything that's not funny. I wanted to get out of there. I had things to do.

Dr. Deal went back inside her office. I stared at the blank piece of paper. Maybe I should tell the truth. I hadn't done my homework because I was watching television. I didn't think Dr. Deal was really going to accept that as an intelligent excuse. I thought about lying, but Dr. Deal hated liars even more than lazy kids who don't do their work. All right, I'd try to be logical. I took my pen and wrote:

I did not do my homework because . . . by the time I got home, I took a rest after a loooong day. I had to have dinner and the pizza guy was late. Then it was eight o'clock. I had to help my grandmother watch Comedy Central. Then it was 8:24. I was going to do my homework, but the TV wouldn't let me. Then I drank hot cocoa for five minutes. By that time it was 9:35. It was time for bed. No more time for homework.

I handed the paper to Ms. Lofti. "I'm done," I said. "I wrote a whole page." Ms. Lofti took the paper. She didn't look very interested. Luckily Dr. Deal wasn't around.

School was finally out for the day. I ran to the coffee shop, where Jimmy told me I could meet him. Jimmy was sitting in a far booth with one of his buddies, an older guy in his twenties. They were staring out the window at a woman with a little brown dog.

"Hey, Jimmy!" I said.

He waved to me to keep quiet.

He and his friend continued to stare at the dog. The dog was cute, but I couldn't see anything that special about it. And the woman wasn't young or anything. The dog sniffed a piece of paper lying in the gutter next to a fire hydrant.

"No, no," muttered Jimmy. "Not on the paper! Not on the paper!"

"What?" I asked. "What's going on?"

"Shut up, kid," said Jimmy. But he said it with a grin.

"Don't tell me to shut up and don't call me kid," I told him.

"All right!" he shouted, suddenly grinning from ear to ear. I wondered if he was grinning because I had stood up to him. Jimmy sometimes plays games with me like that. He'll test me—like in a wrestling match—then he'll tell me he's proud of me when I fight back.

I looked out the window. The dog had peed on the fire hydrant. "Pay up," Jimmy said to his buddy, sitting next to him.

"You had a bet on where the dog would pee?" I asked Jimmy incredulously.

Jimmy smirked. "Any bet you win is a good bet!" he said proudly.

His friend paid up. "Lucky guess," he said disgustedly, and left me and Jimmy alone.

Jimmy stretched out his arms along the back of the booth. He looked like he owned the place. "So, little bro, how are things in the Black Mood

Lagoon?" That's Jimmy's nickname for home. I have to admit it's a pretty good nickname. Not nice, but kind of accurate.

"Things are okay. Grandma misses you a lot."

Jimmy grinned. "Yeah, I bet Mom and Dad miss me too—especially Dad."

"They fight about you," I said. "Maybe that's a sign they miss you."

"Well, when they stick a sign in the window that says, 'Come back, Jimmy. We were wrong to get so mad. All is forgiven,' then I'll believe it."

I knew Mom and Dad, especially Dad, would *never* put up a sign like that. Dad would have to admit that he was wrong, and Dad would rather be right than have Jimmy back.

Jimmy stood up. "Hey, Bobby. Don't look so down," he said. He gave me a little pretend punch on the forearm.

"Are you okay?" I asked him.

"Don't worry about me. I'm loving life since I left home." I didn't exactly believe him, but maybe I just didn't want to believe that he was happier living somewhere else.

"I've got phone calls to make, little bro," said Jimmy. "You'd better run along home. Grandma will be worried about you."

"Can I tell her you send your love?" I asked him.

"Sure," said Jimmy. "You can even tell her I mean it." He gave me a smile. Jimmy's got a great smile.

"What about Mom and Dad?" I couldn't help asking him. "Any messages for them?"

Jimmy looked thoughtful. "How's Mom doing?" he asked.

"She's worried about you," I said. "She wants you home."

Jimmy gave a half laugh, as if he didn't really believe it. "How can you tell? Did she actually express an opinion with Dad around?"

"Mom misses you," I insisted.

"Well, tell her I miss her too, and tell Dad 'Knock, knock' for me."

"Knock, knock, who's there?" I said, playing along.

"Nothing," said Jimmy. "Just say 'Knock, knock.'"

Dad used to teach knock-knock jokes to Jimmy and me. "Remember this one?" I said to Jimmy. "I bet it was the first one you and Dad taught me. Knock, knock."

"Who's there?" said Jimmy, but in a resigned voice.

"Cargo."

A slight smile played on Jimmy's lips. "Cargo who?"

"Car go 'beep, beep,'" I said. "Think back—every time we used to go in a car, we'd say, 'Car go beep, beep.' That was a million laughs."

Jimmy just stared at me. "Yeah, that's our dad—a laugh a minute. I'll see you, kid." I watched Jimmy leave. I tried to think of a knock-knock joke to call him back with—but for once nothing seemed funny.

☺

CHAPTER 3

Knock, knock.
Who's there?
Cook.
Cook Who?
Cuckoo yourself!
I didn't come here to be insulted.

My grandmother was waiting in the apartment for me. I aimed the remote at the TV and turned on the comedy channel. "How was school today?" she asked.

"Not bad. It only scarred me for life—but no fatal wounds yet." I looked to see if Grandma would laugh. She gave me a quarter smile. I once read how Eskimos have about a hundred words for snow. Well, Grandma's got a hundred different smiles and laughs. She's got a deep, hearty belly laugh that is off the Richter scale, and that's my favorite. I love to crack her up.

I reached for my lucky Mets baseball cap and settled in for some serious comedy. Grandma stood in front of me blocking the TV, which isn't hard for her to do. Her body is soft like a pillow. A large pillow. I couldn't see around her.

"Uh, Grandma, excuse me. I'm trying to watch here."

"That hat is getting pretty grungy. I should get you a new one."

"I love this hat. Jimmy gave it to me. It's my lucky hat."

"Do you know who wears the smallest hat?"

I shook my head, but I could tell a joke was coming.

"Narrow-minded people," said Grandma. She sat down next to me on the couch.

I laughed. "You know, Grandma, that's pretty funny." A little smile lifted the corner of Grandma's mouth. She loves it when I tell her she's funny. I got out my notebook and wrote her joke down.

"I saw Jimmy just now. He sends you his love."

Grandma looked very sad. "He shouldn't have to send it. If he feels it, he should come up here and tell me. No matter what." She paused. "I think we should turn off the TV so you can do your homework." She reached for the remote. I held it away from her. The comic on TV was making jokes about nose hair. I just had to listen.

Grandma folded her arms across her ample chest. "Let me see it," she said.

I rolled my eyes. "What?"

"Your homework," she repeated.

"I did it, honest. It was a science project. But we had a problem at school. You've heard about the budget cuts at the Board of Ed? Well, they cut off the gravity at school. Everybody's homework just floated up and flew right out the window."

The creases on Grandma's face started to float upward—just as if gravity really had been reversed. She started to laugh—her big belly laugh. I loved it.

See, that's what I'm good at. Sometimes I come up with a joke, and I don't use it just once. I play with it, trying out different ways to use it— like the best funky music.

Grandma gave me a hug. "You know, honey," she said, chuckling, "sometimes you're too funny for your own good." I hugged her back.

My parents came in the door. If Grandma has a million different smiles and laughs, then Mom and Dad have about as many looks that show they're upset or angry about something. Right now on my mad scale I'd give Mom a seven and Dad an eight. Mom gave me a bright smile—as if everything was just fine—but I just knew she didn't feel that way. Dad's face was easier to read. He was in a bad mood. His shoulders were kind of hunched—like a prizefighter ready to take or throw a punch. *The Black Mood Lagoon* was playing at my local movie theater.

"Don't you have anything better to do than watch television?" Dad asked me.

"Grandma and I haven't just been watching TV," I said. "I've been telling her about a science experiment we did at school. If gravity could get turned off, what would float first?"

"Ha! A lightweight like you would float off in a second," said my father.

Nice, huh? Mom shot Dad a dirty look, but she didn't say anything.

"I'm not a lightweight," I mumbled.

"That's not what your father meant, honey," said my mom. I'd be rich if I had a quarter for every time Mom's said, "You know your father didn't mean it."

"Right, kiddo," said my father. "You know I'm just teasing. Hey, you're the one who likes jokes."

"Bobby saw Jimmy today," Grandma blurted out, changing the subject.

"What did he say?" Mom asked.

"He misses you, Mom," I said. It wasn't exactly a lie.

"Any messages for me?" asked Dad.

"He said to tell you, 'Knock, knock,'" I said.

"Who's there?" asked Dad.

I shrugged. "He just said 'Knock, knock.'"

Dad sighed. "So, Bobby—what kind of trouble did you get in at school today?" I glared at him. He might have guessed right, but it didn't make it any better that he just assumed a day wouldn't go by when I didn't get in trouble.

Dad gave me a knowing look, as if he had hit the bull's-eye. "What was it this time? Did they give you an idiot-proof task and then you proved that someone will always make a better idiot?"

"Hey, who're you calling an idiot?" I asked, knowing exactly who.

"That's mean," said Grandma.

"Yeah, Dad," I said. "It was mean."

Dad looked at me. He didn't apologize. He looked at me shrewdly. "What kind of trouble did you get in at school today?"

"I didn't," I shouted.

"Bobby, don't raise your voice to your father," said Mom.

I didn't even realize that I had been shouting. "Well, tell him not to insult me," I said, trying to lower my voice.

"How did I insult you?" asked Dad, pretending to be innocent.

"You just assumed I was in trouble in school today," I protested. So what if Dad had been right—that wasn't the point. Suddenly I thought of a knock-knock joke that Dad had taught me. "I have a joke for you," I said. "Knock, knock."

"Who's there?" asked Dad, but suspiciously.

"Cook," I said.

"Cook who?" he asked.

"Cuckoo yourself! I didn't come here to be insulted." I laughed, but it wasn't really funny.

"Bobby, how many times do I have to tell you? There's such a thing as being too funny for your own good," said Dad.

"I don't know how many times," I shot back. "But you're obviously going for the record."

"Very amusing," said Dad. But I could tell he didn't think it was.

It's funny—and I don't mean ha-ha funny— that when Grandma or Mr. Matous tells me I'm too funny for my own good, I don't get mad at them. When my father tells me, I want to kill him.

Dad looked at me as if he suspected what was on my mind.

"Don't give me that sneer," he said. "Where are your manners?"

"I gave them the day off," I answered.

"Bobby! Enough is enough," thundered Dad.

I once heard Lily Tomlin, the voice of Ms.

Frizzle, say that "Enough is enough" is one of the lies our parents tell us. I wonder if Dad had ever heard of her.

Mom was looking at Dad and me with a sad expression on her face, but she didn't step in and say anything. Any fight with Dad was an unfair one, and Mom tended to stick to a neutral corner. Instead of doing my homework, I pulled out my notebook filled with jokes. At least on those pages there was no such thing as being too funny for my own good.

☺

CHAPTER 4

Why is it so easy to fool vampires?
Because they're suckers.

The next morning, I was standing on the steps of school in the early-morning sun with Willie, Tyrone and Janeen. "Did you have trouble with the math homework?" Janeen asked.

"It didn't bother me at all. I ignored it." I got a laugh out of Willie, but Janeen didn't laugh.

"Mr. Matous is going to be mad at you again," she said.

"So what?" I said.

"How long are you planning to go without doing any homework?" asked Willie.

I shrugged. "I'm trying for a spot in the *Guinness Book of Records*. I've got a ways to go, I guess."

"Cool," said Willie. "But I bet you don't make it."

"You're on," I said.

"What will we bet?" asked Willie.

"The loser has to go the principal's office." I laughed.

"That's so stupid," said Janeen. "Bobby, you lose either way. If you don't do your homework, you'll have to go to the principal's office any-how."

"Don't call me stupid, Janeen," I said.

"I didn't. I just hate it when you make stupid bets—that's just like your brother."

I can make fun of Jimmy's stupid bets, but I don't like it when anybody outside of the family does—even Janeen. I gave her a dirty look. "Yeah? Well you're so stupid, you think that baby-sitters sit on babies," I blurted at her.

"Thank you very much!" said Janeen. She stomped away, and instantly I felt bad. The baby-sitter joke was funny, but it *was* mean. It just slipped out of my mouth. And Janeen was right. Betting Willie that I could set some kind of record for not doing my homework is exactly the kind of dumb bet Jimmy would make. Sometimes I open my mouth, and words pop out that come straight from Jimmy's brain. That scares me. If I won the bet with Willie, I'd probably get kicked out of school. Jimmy's proof that in my family if you get kicked out of school, you can get kicked out of the house too. I mean, Jimmy left voluntarily, but it doesn't seem that anybody's in a hurry to get him back home again.

I walked into school past Dr. Deal. She looked at me suspiciously. I had a feeling that she didn't appreciate my essay, but she let me pass. In homeroom, Mr. Matous sat on the edge of his desk, his leg jiggling nervously up and down. His shoe beat rhythmically against his desk.

After attendance, Dr. Deal's voice came over the loudspeaker. "Good morning, girls and boys. Your teacher is about to give you an important notice. But before she or he does, here is the thought to ponder today." Dr. Deal always gives us an idea to ponder. They are never funny and almost always boring. "Answers to opinion questions are always right. Now, everyone have a good day."

Mr. Matous looked up at the loudspeaker. He twirled a pencil between his fingers. "All right, class, here's the important announcement. There has been an outbreak of head lice in school. If you do have them, it is nothing to be ashamed of. However, you cannot come back to school until you have been treated with a special shampoo. I have a note for each of you to take home. Head lice have to be treated with the medicine that kills them."

All the kids instantly began feeling their scalps. There were a few groans.

"Oh, yuck! I hate lice," said Sahira, Janeen's friend.

"They're only bugs. They're not gonna kill ya," I argued. "They're just little bugs who have come in peace. All they want to do is to live in our hair. It's not fair to kill them. Where does the SPCA stand on this issue?"

"Bobby," said Mr. Matous, cracking a smile. "I'm glad to see you are taking such a civic interest. However, the school has to maintain a strictly no-head-lice policy and, since no other pets are allowed in school . . ."

That's why I love Mr. Matous. Sometimes he'll take something funny I say and top it. And then I'll try to top that. I've never had a teacher like him before.

"The no-head-lice rule is discrimination," I riffed. "I . . ."

"That's enough about head lice, Bobby," warned Mr. Matous. "Class, I'd like to talk about a more pleasant subject—your next homework assignment."

"Gosh, what's your idea of an *un*pleasant subject?" I asked.

"That's enough, Bobby. I think you'll enjoy this assignment. Adults—politicians, educators, your parents—are always talking about how to improve the schools. Nobody asks you—the students, the consumers. What do *you* think would make school a better place? Let your imagination run free. I want you to write a one-page essay explaining what you would do to improve school if you could do anything you'd like."

"That's easy," I shouted out. "School would be improved if I were made principal. Today, the question of the day to ponder is: Why is it easy to fool vampires?"

"Because they're born suckers," said Mr. Matous, deadpan.

"I didn't know you knew that joke," I said.

"I know a lot of jokes," said Mr. Matous. "But this class isn't a joke contest, so no more interruptions, Bobby. If you genuinely think that having a student as principal would make school a better place, then feel free to write about that. I want you each to give me a logical, well-reasoned suggestion. Perhaps we can take some of the best responses to the school board. Now, speaking of homework, please take out your math homework and pass it to the person on your left."

There was a lot of shuffling of papers as everyone played pass-the-homework—everyone except me, of course.

Sahira raised her hand. "Bobby didn't give me anything," she said.

Mr. Matous glared at me. I was surprised to see him that angry. "Bobby, where's your homework?"

I couldn't think of any snappy comebacks. Telling him I bet Willie that I could make the *Guinness Book of Records* for not doing my homework wasn't going to cut it.

"Did you do it?" Mr. Matous demanded. I shook my head.

"Bobby, I warned you yesterday. You can't get away with not doing your work. Go to Dr. Deal's office, and wait for me." He scribbled a note to her. "I'll be there during my break, and we'll discuss this together."

Janeen gave me a sad look. I knew she felt sorry for me, but I didn't want her pity.

CHAPTER 5

Knock, knock.
Who's there?
Ezra.
Ezra Who?
Ezra any hope for me?

Ms. Lofti looked up from her work when she saw me. "Back so soon, Bobby?" she said. I nodded.

"Let me guess. You didn't do your homework. What's your excuse this time? Aliens took your homework to study the human brain?"

"That's pretty funny," I said.

"I've heard every excuse there is about homework," Ms. Lofti said. "Our puppy paper-trained on it. My little sister ate it. I put it in a safe and forgot the combination."

I laughed. Dr. Deal came out of her office. She didn't look pleased to see me or pleased that

I was laughing with Ms. Lofti. "Bobby, what is it this time?" she demanded.

"Mr. Matous told me to come down here until his break," I said. I gave her Mr. Matous's note.

She read it. "Please sit quietly until Mr. Matous comes down. And don't disturb Ms. Lofti. She has work to do." Dr. Deal handed Ms. Lofti some papers and went back into her office. I tried to sit quietly, but I was worried. It wasn't fun being the kid who always gets in trouble. But I couldn't seem to stop. Maybe it was something in both Jimmy's and my genes that made us poison to schools. Maybe our gene pool could use a little chlorine.

After a while, Mr. Matous came into the front room of the principal's office. He said hello to Ms. Lofti. She offered him a cookie. I noticed that she didn't offer me one. Mr. Matous took a cookie and sat next to me. He has long legs, and they stretched out.

"I'm sorry I made the jokes about the head lice," I said.

"Your jokes are not why you're here. You're here because you won't do your work."

"I didn't do nothing—honest."

"That's exactly the point. And stop using the double negative. 'I didn't do nothing—honest' really means 'I did do something that got me in trouble—honest.' But this isn't about semantics."

"What are semantics?" I said.

"Words. This isn't about words or jokes. I'm worried about you. You're wasting valuable school time that you need to get ahead. Fifth grade is too important to just laugh off."

Just then, Dr. Deal came out of her office. "Mr. Matous, I'm glad you asked for this meeting. I'm as concerned about Bobby as you are. Let's go into my office."

We walked together into Dr. Deal's office. It was a big room with two huge windows that looked out over the playground. Dr. Deal sat behind her desk and motioned Mr. Matous to the couch by the side of her desk. I sat on a hard-backed chair next to the couch. Dr. Deal shuffled some papers on her desk. She seemed to be looking for something. I got a feeling of dread in the bottom of my stomach.

"I made a vow to myself when I became principal of this school that we would not just pass children on to the middle school," said Dr. Deal as if she were talking to a hundred people, not just the two of us. "Bobby is showing serious signs of not being prepared to do the work at a higher level."

I hate it when people talk about me as if I were not even there.

Mr. Matous at least looked at me. "Bobby, Dr. Deal is right. You're bright. You're a live wire in class, and I don't want to squelch that. You've got a unique mind, but you have to start doing the work assigned to you. You can't continue to waste the class's time and mine and yours by ignoring your studies."

Dr. Deal didn't look impressed with his compliments. "Mr. Matous, read what Bobby wrote yesterday as his excuse for not doing his homework." She handed him the piece of paper that she had been looking for. The feeling of dread sank down into my legs. I wish I could have glued down all the papers on Dr. Deal's desk so that she wouldn't be able to hand my essay to Mr. Matous.

"I told the truth. I was even trying to be logical," I argued, as Mr. Matous read it. "Nobody can say I didn't. . . ." I felt as if I were going to cry. "Is that another double negative?"

"No, Bobby, it's not," said Mr. Matous. He folded my paper. I thought I saw a little smile on his face, but then he erased it. "Bobby, you seem to think I assign homework for my own good. I do not. Your homework is your responsibility, and it's for your ultimate benefit—so that you will learn and understand the material being taught."

"The point is that none of your threats to Bobby have worked," insisted Dr. Deal. "I don't think they have teeth in them."

I hated the fact that Mr. Matous seemed to be in trouble because of me. I could just imagine Dr. Deal recommending that Mr. Matous get a giant Doberman pinscher with huge teeth to sic on me.

"I've been thinking of having Bobby reassigned to the School for Intervention," said Dr. Deal.

I blinked. The School for Intervention is for kids with "behavioral problems." And it's all the way across town. Jimmy had to go there. I hated the thought of not finishing out fifth grade with Mr. Matous.

"I don't think the School for Intervention is where Bobby belongs," said Mr. Matous thoughtfully. "I'd like to give him one more chance. I would like to meet with his parents again and see if we can come up with a plan of action."

Dr. Deal interrupted him. "I have seen behavioral problems like Bobby's before. The answer is discipline, discipline, discipline. It's already the beginning of March. By April first, I want to make a decision."

I studied Dr. Deal's face. I knew she had made up her mind already. She didn't want me in her school. Kids like me brought down the school's reputation. Maybe I should save time and ask to be transferred directly to the School for

Troublemakers. Do not pass Go. Do not collect $200. I felt my stomach clench. I wondered if I was going to be sick, right there in her office. It would serve her right if I threw up on her rug.

"What if I promised to do the work?" I found myself begging. "I could try harder. Honest."

Dr. Deal ignored me. She turned to Mr. Matous. "If I give Bobby a brief probationary period, you must work with his parents to make sure that he realizes that continuing this behavior will only get him in trouble."

"I agree," said Mr. Matous.

"All right, Mr. Matous, just so we understand each other. I expect to get a report from you about the plan that you make with Bobby's parents, and I want to hear that he is doing his homework and all his other school assignments, including extra work to make up for what he has refused to do in the past. That will be all."

Mr. Matous stood up. "Come on, Bobby," he said.

We stood in the hall. Mr. Matous took out his notebook and quickly wrote in it. He tore out the page. "I'm giving you a note to take to your parents. I want to meet with all three of you."

"Yes, sir," I said. "My parents are used to kids in trouble. My brother Jimmy's given them plenty of practice."

"You are not your brother," said Mr. Matous.

"You don't even know Jimmy," I said.

He put his arm on my shoulder. I pulled away. I didn't want him to see me cry.

"Bobby, we can turn this thing around, but you're going to have to work with me. You're on your ninth life here. I don't think you belong at the School for Intervention, but you can't keep treating my homework assignments as jokes."

"No, sir," I said. "They aren't that funny."

"Bobby, stop it!" snapped Mr. Matous. "There's got to be a limit, and I am the one who has to set it, not you." He put the note in an envelope and gave it to me. "You will take this note to your parents. Don't even *think* about not giving it to them. I want to hear from them by tomorrow. If not, I will call them myself. I'd like to see them before the end of the week. Tomorrow after school would be ideal."

We walked back up to the classroom together. Ms. Harris, the other fifth-grade teacher, was waiting for him. Mr. Matous left me and went to talk to her. He told her something, and she started to laugh. I didn't like to see Mr. Matous having fun so soon after yelling at me. I had a feeling they were both laughing about me. I put the letter in my backpack.

Somehow I got through the rest of the day. I

can't say I learned a lot. I kept thinking about how my parents would react to the note from Mr. Matous. It was as if the note from Mr. Matous were alive—like something in a horror movie whispering through my backpack, "You're in trouble, buddy, big trouble, and this time you're not getting out of it." The dismissal bell rang. I jumped. It was literally as if the bell had been that creepy voice in my ear.

"What's wrong with you?" asked Janeen.

"Nothing," I said.

"What happened with Dr. Deal?"

"I don't want to talk about it, okay?"

"Was it that bad?"

"Naw, I'm sure I'll love the School for Intervention."

Janeen looked stricken, but I really didn't want to talk about it. We passed the open door to the teachers' room. I could hear Ms. Krosnick laughing. She's one of the fourth-grade teachers. She's got a really loud laugh—like a donkey bray. Then Ms. Krosnick said something, and I heard Mr. Matous give a huge belly laugh. I wondered what they were all laughing at.

"The teachers are having a blast," I said to Janeen. "Do you think they're having a joke contest—who can tell the funniest story about Bobby messing up?" I heard more laughing coming from the teachers' room. This time it sounded as if it Ms. Lorenzo was telling them something funny. Maybe they were really trying to outdo one another to see who had the funniest stories—not just about me, but about all the kids who mess up in school. I really wished I could hear what they were saying.

Janeen ignored the laughing. How could she do that? Whenever I hear anybody laughing, even strangers on the street, I always want to know why.

"Come on, Bobby," Janeen insisted. "Tell me what happened in the principal's office. Did she really say she wanted to send you to the School for Intervention?"

"Drop it, okay? I'm trying to find out what the teachers think is so funny. I think they're having a laugh-off."

"What's a laugh-off?" asked Janeen.

"Nothing," I said. "I just made that up. But it sounds like fun. More fun than being kicked out of school. Maybe I should see if we can get invited."

"Bobby, let's go home," urged Janeen. "We're not supposed to hang around outside the teachers' room."

The laughter got louder. Ms. Harris said something that cracked them all up. I could hear them trading stories back and forth. And I was sure some of them were about me. I couldn't help myself. I knocked on the doorframe. Ms. Krosnick came to the door.

"What do you want?" she asked. She didn't seem happy to see me.

"Is Mr. Matous there?" I asked.

Mr. Matous came to the door. "What is it, Bobby?" he asked.

"Knock, knock," I said weakly.

"Who's there?" said Mr. Matous.

"Ezra," I said.

"Ezra who?"

"Ezra any hope for me?"

Mr. Matous didn't laugh. I don't know why I expected him to. I guess teachers don't have to laugh at kids' jokes after school hours.

"Bobby, go home," said Mr. Matous. "I know this has been a tough day for you, but you've got to face the music sometime. And you know you're not allowed in the teachers' room."

"I just wanted to know what the laughing was all about," I said.

"Go home," repeated Mr. Matous. I didn't want to.

CHAPTER 6

😁

What did one flea say to the other?
"Shall We Walk, or Shall We take the dog?"

"You have a note from your teacher. You got in trouble today, didn't you?"

I swear—those were the first words Grandma said to me when I walked in the door. I hadn't said a word. Maybe I'd been right—that note in my backpack was alive and giving off a noise audible to me and Grandma: "He's in trouble! He's got a note from school!"

I suddenly realized that I had two notes in my knapsack, and that maybe I could do a switch. At least it would buy me some time. "I do have a note from the teacher, but I'm not in trouble. Some kid got head lice, and now we all have to be checked."

"Oh no, not lice! Once when I was a kid, I touched my best friend's braid and I got head lice and they made me shave my hair," said

Grandma. "I had to wear a wig. I was so humili-
ated. Let me look."

I bent down my head for her inspection. Her
fingers felt gentle on my scalp. "There's one little
louse," said Grandma, parting my hair. "He's
kind of cute. I think he's doing the jitterbug."

I hooted. "Grandma! That's so funny. Did
you just think that up?"

Grandma nodded, and I could tell she was
pleased that I liked her joke. "Well, that little bug
is certainly doing some kind of dance," she said.

"In class today, I told the teacher that head
lice have a right to live too."

"Not on my grandson's head," said Grandma.
"Come on." She went to the medicine cabinet
and got down the awful-smelling shampoo. She
put on yellow rubber gloves. "The doctor is ready
to operate," she said.

"Maybe we should let them dance a little
more," I said. "Poor guys. They're having a
party. Suddenly it's a raid, and the shampoo
police are there."

"I suppose we could let them have one last
dance before they go," said Grandma. "Maybe
we should put some music on for them."

Grandma put her backside in motion as she
did a little two-step over to the stereo and put on
some of her favorite New Orleans music.

Grandma grew up in New York City, but she says her soul is from New Orleans. She held out her hands for me to dance with her. We've been dancing together ever since I can remember.

She studied my hair as we danced. "Oh look," she said. "There's one doing the electric slide. He's a funky little bug. There's another one—that one's doing the Macarena." Grandma and I both started waving our hands in the air and shaking our hips. We did a quarter turn and then I started laughing so hard, I collapsed in a heap on the floor.

Grandma smiled down at me. "Your grandfather used to laugh like that. I could make him laugh until tears rolled down his face."

I looked up at her. "I love to make *you* laugh," I said.

"I know," said Grandma.

"So if Grandpa loved to laugh, and you love to laugh, how come Dad . . ." I paused. I didn't know what to say. I know Dad thinks he's funny, but he isn't.

Grandma looked at me as if she understood. "Your grandfather had a lot of rules," she said. "I could make your grandfather laugh, but he wanted his son to know that life wasn't a bed of roses." She shook her head and sighed.

It was weird for me to think of Dad as a kid

with problems with his own dad. I never met my grandfather. He died before I was born. Dad always seems so sure of himself, sure that he is right. So sure about rules.

"Come on. Let me shampoo your hair," said Grandma, cheering up again. We went into the bathroom. I sat on the toilet while she rubbed the shampoo on my head. It burned a little, and it stank. "Good-bye, poor little lice," I said. I held my head over the sink, and Grandma rinsed the shampoo out, careful not to get it in my eyes. I watched the shampoo go down the drain.

"Let's say something nice about lice," said Grandma.

We both broke up laughing before we could think of anything. Then we heard the front door open. Dad shouted, "Anybody home?" Grandma and I looked at each other.

"We're in the bathroom," shouted Grandma.

"What's that smell?" Dad followed the smell into the bathroom where we were.

"It's louse shampoo," said Grandma.

My father scratched his head, just the way all of us did when Mr. Matous mentioned the little critters. I smiled.

"What's so funny?"

"Nothing. You were just scratching your hair.

That's what everybody does when they hear about head lice."

"That's all we need," said Dad. "Lice in the house. Jimmy moves out so you decided to bring us a little house pet? Is that it, Bobby?"

"The head lice are not Bobby's fault," said Grandma.

"How can you talk about a pet replacing Jimmy?" I said angrily. "I miss him. Jimmy's still my brother."

The funky, jitterbugging lice were deader than a doornail. The laughing and the dancing seemed to belong to another planet. Grandma wiped her hands and started to leave the bathroom. Dad made room for Grandma to pass, but they gave each other a funny look. Sometimes it's hard for me to remember that Grandma is my dad's mother. The two of them are so incredibly different.

Dad leaned on the doorframe of the bathroom. "I just remembered a bug joke," he said to me. "What did one flea say to the other flea?"

"'Shall we walk, or shall we take the dog?'" I answered. Dad told me that joke a long time ago.

"Naw. 'Shall we walk, or shall we take the kid with bugs in his ears?'"

"Dad, I don't get that joke. It doesn't make sense."

"Well, you're the kid with a bug in his ear."

"I don't have bugs in my ears. They were in my hair."

"Don't be so literal. You're losing your sense of humor," said Dad.

I could tell Dad was trying to tell me a joke to smooth over what he had said about Jimmy, but a joke wasn't the same as saying he was sorry.

"What about your homework, Bobby?" said Dad. "Have you done it, or do you have a bug in your ear about that too?"

"I'd like to put a bug in your ear," I muttered, just low enough so that he didn't understand.

"What's that?" Dad asked suspiciously.

I thought about the note from Mr. Matous. I could feel it pulsing like an obnoxious beeper in my backpack. I didn't want to give it to Dad—not now, not ever. "I don't have a bug in my ear," I said, just wanting to say anything that would get the subject away from homework. "Who gets bugs in their ears anyhow?"

"It's just a thing kids say," Dad said, as if he were the authority on what kids say.

"No kids I know say it," I said.

"Yeah, well, the kids you know probably think bungee jumping off the Empire State Building should be an Olympic sport."

"That's not true," I said.

"Didn't you want to go bungee jumping this summer?"

"Yes, with Tyrone and his father. They said it was perfectly safe. And it wasn't off the Empire State Building, it was from a crane on one of the piers."

"And if Tyrone wanted you to jump off a bridge, would you do it?"

I sighed. I hated that question. Dad was always asking it—as if it made sense and was the perfect reason for saying no whenever I asked to do something my friends got to do.

Dad looked at me. "Well, you didn't answer my question."

"About jumping off a bridge?"

"No. About doing your homework."

"I did it," I lied. "Now, excuse me. I want to wash the smell of the shampoo off."

Dad gave me a funny look but left the bathroom. I wondered if he had inherited Grandma's extrasensory powers and knew that I had a note from Mr. Matous.

I went into the shower. I turned the water on as hot as I could stand it. My body's changing on me. I'm getting bigger—all over. I'm about three inches taller than I was at the beginning of the school year. I was nearly five foot three even though I was only in fifth grade. Dad was only five foot seven. Maybe by sixth grade I'll be taller than him. I let the water run over me. Maybe I could just stay in the shower until that happened.

CHAPTER 7

😉

What's round and has a bad temper?
A Vicious circle.

Dinner that night was not exactly a barrel of laughs. In fact, I can't remember a word that was said. I know what words didn't get said: "Mom, Dad—my teacher wants to see you." Every time I tried to get the words out, I felt like I was choking.

Mom noticed that I didn't have my usual appetite. "Are you feeling okay, Bobby?" she asked. "Is something wrong?"

"Maybe the smell of the shampoo gave him a headache," said Grandma.

I just couldn't get up the courage to give my parents the note from Mr. Matous. I decided to sleep on it, but that wasn't a good idea either. I had trouble getting to sleep, and when I finally did, I slept like I was dead. No dreams, nothing.

At six thirty A.M., the alarm went off. I put my head under the pillow and fell back asleep. The next thing I knew, Dad was shaking me so hard I practically fell out of bed.

"Leave me alone. I just got up yesterday," I mumbled.

My father looked down at me. He had a little smile on his face as if he were enjoying himself. I wanted to wipe it off his face. He stripped the covers off the bed. "Get up."

I opened one eye. "Two minutes," I begged him.

"Now," Dad said. "How did you get so lazy?" he demanded.

"Practice, practice, practice," I told him. Dad stomped out of the room.

"Is Bobby up?" I heard Mom ask.

"Let me put it this way. He doesn't have any covers on his bed, and his eyes are open."

"The boy does hate to get up in the morning," said Grandma.

"Jimmy could never get out of bed and get to school on time, and Grandma, you coddled him," said Mom. "You always let him sleep late. I'm trying not to do that with Bobby."

"You say that," said Dad. "But who is it who always has to drag Bobby out of bed? Me. Why don't you try it for a change?"

I pulled the covers back over my head. It was cozy in there. I wished I could stay there all day. I didn't even hear footsteps come into the room. The next thing I knew, something cold and wet was dripping on me. Mom was standing over me with a wet washcloth—a wet, cold washcloth. "Okay, Bobby. Out of bed! Now! Or do you want a wet washcloth in the face?"

"Mom! What are you doing?" I stared at her.

"Your father gave me a challenge," she said.

"Cut it out, Mom. This is scary." She'd never done anything this drastic before.

"I want you to get out of bed and get ready for school."

"Are you trying to prove that you can be just as tough as Dad?" I groaned, rolling away to avoid the dripping washcloth.

"Bobby," warned Mom, "don't give me any of your back talk."

Why do they always call it back talk when you tell them the truth? "I'll rise, but I won't shine."

"Enough jokes," said Mom, but she actually smiled. "Will you get dressed? Or do you want me to do it?"

I wasn't about to have Mom dress me. I shook my head and got out of bed.

"Hey Ma, was that a joke?" I asked her.

"Just get dressed," she said. Suddenly she

sounded tired once again. Once she left the room, I got dressed in record time. When I got to the kitchen, Grandma handed me a glass of orange juice. "Good morning, Bobby," she said.

"Morning, Grandma." I gave her a kiss on the cheek.

"So, what's on the agenda at school for you today?" asked Dad. He made it sound like school was an office. "Are you going to do any work for a change?"

"I do plenty of work," I mumbled. I was sick of his sarcasm, but I was sick about something else too. I knew I had to give Mom and Dad the note from Mr. Matous. Most of the time, Mr. Matous doesn't sound like other adults, but when he said, "Don't even think about not giving them the note," I knew I had crossed a line. Mr. Matous would never let me pretend that I had lost the note. He'd call my parents himself and tell them everything.

"Uh, Mom, Dad," I mumbled, "my teacher wants to see you."

As if all the molecules in the room had stopped moving, Mom and Dad just froze and looked at each other. Then I tried to hand the note to Mom, but Dad took it.

"I didn't do nothing," I said as Dad read it.

Dad glared at me. "You don't even know how

to speak English," he said. "No wonder you're failing at school."

"I know how to talk," I mumbled. I realized that I had slipped and said the same stupid double thing that Mr. Matous had talked about. "I just made a mistake."

Dad read Mr. Matous's note. "I think, young man, you've made more than one mistake. You seem to think the rules apply to everyone but you. You've been lying to us, saying that you've done your homework."

I cringed. I *had* lied to him. This wasn't the time to tell him that I had a bet with Willie to see if I could make the *Guinness Book of Records*.

"Tell your teacher that I'll be there today at three o'clock," said Dad. "I'll have to get someone to cover me at work, but I'll be there. You'll cost me money, but I'll be there."

He hadn't even asked Mom if she could come at that time. Mom played with her napkin. "What time did you say again?" she asked into the air, as if she weren't really sure who she was asking. She was far different from the character who had stood over my bed with a wet washcloth. I almost liked that person better.

"Three o'clock," said my father. His teeth were clenched. He really didn't care whether Mom came or not.

"I'll try to be there," she said. "Bobby, I'm so disappointed. I thought . . ." Her voice trailed off. Mom often didn't finish sentences.

Dad finished this one for her. "Your mother thought that you were different from Jimmy. But you keep going out of your way to prove to us both that she's wrong."

"I'm not Jimmy. I screw up in my own way."

"And you think that's something to be proud of?" said my father.

I didn't even know why I bothered opening my mouth. Like Dr. Deal, my father had made up his mind about me long ago.

"Do you want to hear a joke, Bobby?" asked Dad.

I was sure he was going to come out with something sarcastic about my not doing my homework or that I was just like Jimmy. I wish I had bet on it. I would have won.

"What's round and has a bad temper?" he asked.

"I don't know," I mumbled.

"A vicious circle!" said my father.

"I don't get it," I said.

"A vicious circle is when you keep repeating the same mistake over and over and over again and can't stop."

"That joke's nasty," I shouted at him.

"It's mean *and* vicious."

"Bobby, don't raise your voice to your father," said Mom.

"Bobby's right," said Grandma. "That joke had a nasty edge. It was a cruel thing to say to your son."

"I thought you and Bobby liked jokes," said Dad, sounding disgusted. He got up and threw his napkin on the table.

Ah, breakfast time at the Garrick house. Snap, crackle, pop.

CHAPTER 8

Knock, knock.

Who's there?

Lester.

Lester Who?

Lester over a new leaf.

I got out of there as soon as I could. I went down-stairs and rang Janeen's bell. We live in the same apartment building and have been going to school together since first grade.

"I'll be ready in a minute," said Janeen. "I was just going over my essay for how to improve the school. Did you do it?"

I shook my head. "I had a tough night. Grandma shampooed my hair with Nix. We let the head lice have one last dance. What do you call nervous insects?"

"Jitterbugs?" said Janeen tentatively. She smiled at me. She's always so happy when she gets a joke.

"You got it!" I said.

Janeen's mom came into the living room. "Hi, Bobby," she said, smiling. She's nice, but I wasn't in the mood for parents. "Hi," I said. "Let's go, Janeen. You can look over your essay in school, before class starts."

"Okay," Janeen said. She put on her parka. The March wind was cold.

"How come last winter we had a million snow days, and this year, when I need them, we haven't had any?" I asked.

"Why do you need one?" asked Janeen.

"Because if we had a snow day, then my parents wouldn't be coming to school to talk about my little homework problem," I said.

"It's not a *little* homework problem," said Janeen. "It's a big problem."

"Come on, Janeen." I tried to tease her. "I told Willie and the other kids I was going for the world's record, remember?"

"Bobby Garrick, do you *want* to get kicked out of school?" Janeen demanded.

I thought about Dad's joke. "It's a vicious circle," I said.

"What does that mean?" asked Janeen.

"It's a private joke between my dad and me."

"Well, I won't think it's funny when you get transferred to the School for Intervention. I'll miss you." Janeen just said what she was feeling straight out. That's what I love about her. There's nothing fake about Janeen. She may not be the funniest person, but whatever she feels, she's not afraid to say it. Besides, I probably wouldn't want a best friend who was funnier than me.

When we got to school, it was still pretty early. A bunch of teachers were standing in the hall holding coffee cups. Mr. Matous was at the center of them. Ms. Harris said something, and Mr. Matous laughed. Then Mr. Matous said something to her, and she cracked up. Mr. Matous was just standing there laughing, and my life was falling apart—all because of his note. Mr. Matous said something else to the teachers, and then he laughed again.

I turned to Janeen. "Have you ever noticed that every time you see a group of teachers together without any kids, they're laughing? There should be a rule that when the teachers laugh, they have to tell us what they're laughing about."

Janeen chuckled. "I like that rule. You should have written that for your homework assignment on how to improve the school," she said.

Willie and Tyrone came up to us. "Hey Bobby, what's up? Still going for the world's record?" asked Willie.

"Lay off, Willie," said Janeen. "If Bobby doesn't start doing his homework, he'll get kicked out of school."

"So did you do your homework?" Willie asked me.

I shook my head. "Naw."

Before I could say any more, Janeen chimed in. "But he just had a really great idea, and if he hurries, he can do it before school starts."

"Yeah, Bobby," teased Willie. "You'd better do what the teacher's pet tells you to do. Especially if she's your girlfriend."

I hate it when kids tease us about being boyfriend and girlfriend. We aren't. I also wished Janeen would stop going on and on about the homework, especially in front of the guys.

"Is that a yellow streak I see growing on your back?" asked Tyrone. "You turning chicken and going to do your homework?" He began to cluck like a chicken.

"Shut up, Tyrone," said Janeen. "You do your homework. So does Willie. You two aren't the ones in trouble."

"Janeen, you really *are* such a teacher's pet," said Willie.

I wanted to stick up for Janeen, like she always did for me. But Janeen does take everything so seriously, and I know a lot of the other kids do think she is the teacher's pet. I could see Willie waiting for me to come up with a zinger.

"Let's see, Janeen." I pretended to ponder. "The assignment was what to do to improve the school. Why don't they expel all the teachers' pets instead of the class clowns? That would improve school." I laughed to show her that I just wanted the guys to stop teasing us about being boyfriend and girlfriend.

Janeen looked hurt and mad.

"Hey, I was just kidding," I said.

"As if that makes everything all right!" she yelled. "Do you know what I wrote, Bobby Garrick? I wrote that we should have a rule against put-downs. But that would put you out of business."

"My father's the master of put-downs, not me," I protested.

"Oh yeah? How about telling me that I'm so stupid I think baby-sitters sit on babies? Or that the best way to improve the school would be to expel me?"

"But you know I was kidding!" I said.

"I told you. That doesn't make me feel better," said Janeen.

"Lighten up, Janeen," said Willie. "Bobby was just being funny."

"Shut up, Willie," I said. I *had* put Janeen

down, and then made it worse by saying 'Only kidding.' When Dad did that to me, I wanted to murder him. I was turning into some kind of Frankenstein monster—half Jimmy, half Dad. Yeech!

"You two are weird," said Willie.

Janeen glared at me. "Nobody cares about your stupid brag that you weren't going to do your homework. Willie did his homework." She looked over at him. "Didn't you?"

"I wrote about improving the food at the cafeteria," said Willie.

"How original," Janeen said.

"That's a put-down," I pointed out.

Janeen made a face. "So I made a little one. I'm sorry, Willie."

"Hey, why are you two are making such a big deal out of this?" asked Willie. "Bobby's put-downs are hilarious. And Bobby, I think it's funny that you're not doing your homework. I mean, I wouldn't want to put any real money down on whether you make the record, but—"

"See?" said Janeen. "That's what's so stupid about some of your bets, Bobby. You make them, and nobody cares."

The warning bell rang. Mr. Matous made a parting joke to Mrs. Harris and the other teachers. We had fifteen minutes before school started.

"I'm going up early," said Janeen. I followed her into the classroom.

"I didn't mean that joke about your being the teacher's pet," I said to her. "It just slipped out."

"I know," she said. "But that doesn't make me feel any better."

"I'm sorry," I said.

Janeen blinked. "You hardly ever say you're sorry."

"Well, I am," I said. I couldn't tell if she believed me or not.

"Knock, knock," I said to her.

"Who's there?" she asked, but as if she wasn't really interested.

"Lester," I said.

"Lester who?

"Lester over a new leaf." I gave her a half smile. Janeen rolled her eyes, but I thought she had half forgiven me at least.

Mr. Matous was standing by his desk when we walked into class. "Good morning, Bobby, Janeen. How are you two?"

"I'm fine, Mr. Matous," said Janeen. Something in the clipped way she said the words made me feel that saying I was sorry hadn't really done the trick, and neither had the knock-knock joke. She had emphasized the word "I" as if she wanted to make it clear that we weren't a "we."

"Bobby, did you give your parents my note?" asked Mr. Matous.

Five minutes ago, he had been standing around with the other teachers laughing his head off, not even worried that his note had ruined my life. "Yes, sir," I said. I was aware that my words sounded as clipped as Janeen's. "My father and mother will be here at three o'clock."

Mr. Matous looked up. I almost never called him sir. He seemed to be thinking hard. He didn't say anything for a long moment. When I looked into his eyes, they seemed kind. "Bobby, you have the power to turn this thing around, but it's up to you." He walked away from me as the rest of the class filed in. I was pretty sure that the School for Intervention did not have teachers who liked to laugh.

I took out my notebook. I still had a few minutes before class. I wrote,

The one thing that would most improve school would be a LAUGH-OFF!

I showed the paper to Janeen. "See? I did my homework."

"It's supposed to be a whole page. And you weren't supposed to do the assignment in the two seconds before school starts. That's why they call it homework."

"Janeen," I whispered, "I hope you don't take this as a put-down, but sometimes you really do sound like a miniature adult."

"I'm not a miniature anything," said Janeen. "I'm me."

I smiled at her, because hearing her talk like that, I knew she had forgiven me, at least sort of. I took the paper back and got down to work.

☺

CHAPTER 9

What's a pie in the sky?

A flying pizza.

Mr. Matous stood in front of his desk. "Okay everybody. I want each of you to read your essay. And then we can discuss your ideas."

I folded my hands in front of me on my desk. I looked around. It was hard for me to keep quiet. I felt very nervous.

"Let's start with Priscilla."

I listened to Priscilla's essay. "I think we should give out awards for neatness," she read. "A neat environment is a safe environment. Many kids today think that being messy is cool. I think the school would be improved if we all wore uniforms and if the uniforms were very, very neat. Thank you." Priscilla sat down.

"Very good, Priscilla. Class, any comments?"

I raised my hand. "Maybe we could get uniforms for the head lice too. Boy head lice could wear little blazers and ties, and the girl head lice could wear those little pleated skirts."

Mr. Matous let a smile play around his lips.

"I didn't write it to be funny," said Priscilla.

"I know," said Mr. Matous. "Priscilla, yours was a very good idea. Bobby was just trying to improve on it. Even if his idea wasn't very practical."

"It wouldn't take much material," I added.

Mr. Matous shook his head gently at me. I could tell he was trying to tell me not to take it too far. I didn't want it to seem as if I was putting Priscilla down. I tried to keep quiet.

Tyrone's essay was about improving cafeteria food by ordering out for pizza every day.

"Your idea will never fly," I said. "It's just pie in the sky—pizza pie in the sky."

Tyrone looked angry at me. I guessed I shouldn't have made that joke so fast. I was getting impatient for my turn. Mr. Matous called on Janeen.

"I think we should have a put-down fund," read Janeen. "Every time someone says a put-down, they would have to put in a quarter. Kids think talking trash is fun, but it hurts, and sometimes when someone puts you down all the time, you begin to believe it—that's what my mom and dad say."

I felt as if Janeen were talking straight to me.

"Janeen's suggestion stinks," said Willie. "She just wants that rule because she's such a goody-goody."

"Willie owes Janeen a quarter!" I shouted out. "That's a put-down!"

"You always stick up for Janeen," said Willie. "You think whatever she does is perfect." I loved it that Willie thought I always stuck up for Janeen. Just this morning, I'd felt like I always let her down. I tried to catch Janeen's eye, but she wouldn't look up. I know Janeen. Willie had hurt her feelings. She knows that some kids think she's a goody-goody. I think half the reason she likes me so much is that I'm not a goody-goody. Like some of my badness rubs off on her.

"Willie," said Mr. Matous, "Bobby was right. You shouldn't have told Janeen her idea stinks. I don't want to hear that kind of comment about anyone's ideas. Janeen's idea was very original. That's what I'm looking for."

"I have more suggestions," said Janeen.

"Let's hear from the others first," said Mr. Matous gently. "Okay, Bobby. You seem anxious to tell us about your idea. You're next."

I walked to the front of the room. I unfolded my paper carefully and read it.

I think that the one thing that would most improve school would be a LAUGH-OFF! The teachers should have to tell the kids what they're always laughing at in the teachers' room and in the hals, and the kids would have to tell out loud some of the things we laugh at. It could be a contest.

There were a bunch of snickers.

"Hey, Bobby—there goes your world record," shouted Tyrone.

Mr. Matous looked curious. "What world record?" he asked.

"Bobby was going for the *Guinness Book of Records* for not doing his homework," said Tyrone. "And now he won't get it."

I gave Tyrone a dirty look. "Just shut up," I muttered.

"But I thought you wanted all us kids to tell our jokes in front of the teachers, and vice versa," teased Tyrone.

I turned beet red.

"It's okay, Bobby," said Mr. Matous. "I kind of like your idea. It's very interesting."

I wondered if "interesting" was a put-down.

CHAPTER 10

He's smarter than he looks.
But then he'd have to be.

I couldn't concentrate for the rest of the day. My parents were coming in at three o'clock, and I knew that whatever happened between Mr. Matous and my parents, it wasn't going to be good. At least Janeen wasn't mad at me anymore. I guess the fact that I had stood up for her in class helped. She tried to cheer me up at lunch. She was eating pizza, potato chips, and salad with Thousand Island dressing. Janeen can eat and eat, and she never gains any weight. "Are you going to throw that out?" she asked, eyeing my half-eaten pizza hungrily.

I shoved my pizza toward her. "Who's going to give you their lunch when I'm gone?"

"Where are you going?"

"To the School for Intervention. Where do they come up with these names?"

"Mr. Matous doesn't want to send you there," said Janeen. She sounded absolutely sure.

"Maybe," I said. "But Dr. Deal does, and she's the boss. You know what's the weirdest thing? I don't even know why I stopped doing my homework. It just kind of happened. It's not that I love homework, but I used to do it, didn't I?"

"Yeah, last year, you did your homework. Are you scared about this meeting with Mr. Matous and your parents?" she asked.

"Wouldn't you be?" I asked. "Never mind. It would never happen to you. The only way your parents would get called in would be if you won an award for good citizenship."

"Is that a put-down?" asked Janeen suspiciously.

"I meant it as a compliment. I wish you could go into that meeting instead of me. My mother likes you. She thinks you're a good influence."

"Well, I am," said Janeen. "See—sometimes it's good to hang around with the teacher's pet." She gave me a broad smile just to show me she was teasing.

I smiled at her. "So, O Great Wise One, do you have any advice for what I should do at this meeting with my parents?"

"Keep your mouth shut," said Janeen. "Try just listening for a change."

"Are you saying that I don't listen?"

"Sometimes you don't," said Janeen seriously. "Sometimes when we're talking, you're just waiting to get your next joke in."

"Thanks—any other criticisms to make me feel better?" I asked.

"Nope," said Janeen. She grinned at me.

I wasn't in the mood for jokes. Maybe this was what it felt like being around me all the time. "Was your thing about put-downs . . . were you thinking of me when you wrote it?" I asked her.

"Actually, no. Somehow, with you, I always know that deep down your jokes aren't mean."

"And I know that deep down you're not a goody-goody," I told her. I never talk to anybody, not even Grandma, the way I do to Janeen. I couldn't stand the thought of being put in a school away from her.

I made it through the afternoon. My parents showed up early. They were waiting outside Mr. Matous's locked room as we came up from the computer lab. It was only two forty-five P.M.

My father shook hands with Mr. Matous. "I understand you want to see us," my father said formally. My mother stood next to him looking nervous.

"I do," said Mr. Matous. "If you'll just wait a minute for the dismissal bell, the four of us can meet privately."

My father seemed annoyed at the wait. He scowled as he looked at the bulletin boards. I had a poem up there. It was called "Ode to Road Kill," and Mr. Matous had laughed out loud when I had read it to the class.

> *They look into cars' headlights and their feet turn*
> *to lead*
> *They turn to get away, but boom, they're dead*
> *So when you're driving down Highway 37*
> *You may see animals who've gone to heaven*

I got uncomfortable as I watched Dad read my poem. Janeen also had a poem on the bulletin board. It was about loving to eat.

"Hello, Janeen," said Mom. "I noticed that you have a poem up on the bulletin board. It's lovely."

"Everybody liked Bobby's poem the best," said Janeen. "Me too!"

"Ah, yes—'Ode to Road Kill,'" said Dad. "It sounds familiar. Where did you get it from, Bobby? One of those comedy shows that you always watch on TV?"

"I made it up," I told him.

Mr. Matous came up to my parents. "Why don't we all take a seat," he said. "Janeen, I'll see you tomorrow." Mr. Matous gently ushered her out and closed the door to the classroom. My parents sat awkwardly at two of the desks in the front of the room. Mr. Matous perched on the edge of his desk. I took my seat at my desk halfway back. "Come on up to the front, Bobby," said Mr. Matous.

I shuffled up to one of the front-row desks. Mr. Matous looked serious. "Let me come directly to the point," he said. "Dr. Deal is considering transferring Bobby to the School for Intervention because of the fact that he is not doing his work. I would like to try to find a way to keep Bobby here."

"Bobby, Bobby," said Mom, shaking her head. I don't know why she thought repeating my name was going to help. Maybe she thought I had forgotten who I was.

"The problem is that Bobby thinks everything is a joke," said my father.

"It's not Bobby's humor that bothers me," said Mr. Matous. "In fact, I think it's one of his strengths."

My father looked as if he had just tasted something rotten.

"My wife and I are worried," said my father. "We don't want Bobby to end up expelled from school like his brother, but we're at our wits' end.

We don't know what to do with him."

"It's not like Jimmy's a murderer or anything," I argued. "You didn't have to kick him out of the house."

"I want to keep this focused on Bobby, not his brother," said Mr. Matous firmly. "Bobby, you show great originality, and I want to build on that. You've got to learn to do the hard work that will take advantage of your originality. Your poem on road kill was a great example. I know you worked on that poem."

"I think he got that off a TV show," said Dad.

"I did not!" I shouted.

Mr. Matous looked impatient. "Let's talk about a more current example. Today's home-work assignment."

"I bet he didn't do it," said Dad.

Now Dad sounded like Jimmy. "You'd lose that bet," I said furiously.

"You *would* lose that bet, Mr. Garrick," said Mr. Matous. "Bobby did today's homework, and it was very original . . . as far as it went."

He showed my paper to my parents. My father shook his head. "He couldn't even spell a simple word like 'halls' right. What do you teach them in this school?"

"It's a rough draft," said Mr. Matous.

My father showed my paper to my mother. "I

don't understand," she said. "What's a laugh-off?"

"Bobby," said Mr. Matous, "explain it to your parents and me. What is this laugh-off?"

"I made it up," I said. "Me and Janeen heard you teachers laughing. We always hear you laughing in the teachers' room and in the halls."

"Janeen and I," corrected Dad. "I would think you'd at least try to teach these children grammar."

"Go on, Bobby," said Mr. Matous. "You and Janeen heard the teachers laughing. How did you get from there to a laugh-off?"

I shrugged. I wasn't sure what Mr. Matous wanted from me. "It was a goof. I'm sorry. I shouldn't have written it down. Give me another chance. I'll write something serious."

Mr. Matous played with a pencil. He rolled it up and down his fingers. It was a habit he had. "I think you've already got the beginnings of a good idea. Suppose I give you an assignment to create a laugh-off."

"But I have no idea what a laugh-off is," I protested. "I don't think there's ever been one."

"Make it real," said Mr. Matous seriously. "If you want to prove that you belong in this school, you're going to have to go the extra mile. Put on a laugh-off."

My father exploded. "You're going to encourage him to make more jokes? What in the world for?"

"The newest educational theories encourage us to explore our many types of intelligence," said Mr. Matous. "I think organizing a laugh-off will present Bobby with an interesting challenge. I want to see him use his humor in a constructive way."

"Uh, excuse me," I had to interrupt. "This isn't fair. Why should I have to do more work than anybody else?"

"Because you have refused to do the work that your classmates have done all along," said Mr. Matous. "This is what we discussed with Dr. Deal."

He had me there.

"So are we clear?" Mr. Matous turned to include my parents and me. Mom, as usual, had hardly opened her mouth. "Bobby, for the next month you are in a probationary period," continued Mr. Matous. "During this time you will need to complete all your regular assignments and come up with a laugh-off. I'm looking forward to seeing what you accomplish."

I studied his face. Was the laugh-off a trap? Mr. Matous wasn't the kind of person who set traps. A laugh-off. Pull off a laugh-off. I had to admit that it sounded fun—if I could figure out what it was.

"I don't see what you're going to accomplish," said my father. "We can try to help him. But we can't do it for him."

"I don't *want* you to do it for him," said Mr. Matous forcefully. "You can check his homework for him, make sure he's done it. But that's all."

"Don't worry. I intend to do that," said my father.

"Good," said Mr. Matous. "Bobby is smart enough. He just has to apply himself and find his own way to use his talents."

My father looked at me. "I know he's smarter than he looks," he said. He gave a little laugh. "But then he'd have to be."

Mom gasped softly, but she still didn't say anything. I dug my fingernails into my fists. I remembered my promise to Janeen to listen. But oh, Dad was making me angry. Mr. Matous was studying me. Somehow I felt he was proud that I was keeping my mouth shut.

Mr. Matous stood up to indicate that the meeting was over. I got the feeling that he'd had enough of us. There really wasn't much more to say after my father's comment. My parents got up to leave. "Your grandmother is waiting for you at home," said my father.

I got up to leave with Mom and Dad. "Wait, Bobby," said Mr. Matous. "If you have the time, I'd like to talk to you alone." I felt exhausted. I didn't want to talk anymore, but I felt that Mr. Matous just didn't want to let me go.

My parents left the room.

"Bobby, I know this year has been hard on your parents and you," said Mr. Matous. Obviously he was referring to Jimmy.

I wondered what Mr. Matous had thought of Mom and Dad. Mom had looked tired, but she looked tired a lot these days. Even Dad had looked a little green around the gills. Suddenly I felt protective of them both. I didn't want Mr. Matous telling me what terrible parents they were. Last year in fourth grade, we did *West Side Story*, the musical, and I sang in the chorus. I was one of the Jets, and we sang a great song to a policeman, "Dear Officer Krupke." It was about all the excuses adults believe for why kids get in trouble. The truth, is we don't need excuses. We just do it.

"It's not Mom and Dad's fault I'm in trouble," I said. "I work at that by myself."

"You certainly do. No one can say you're lazy."

"Thanks, Mr. Matous," I said. "Quite a few teachers have said exactly that. But you know what I always say. Hard work has a future payoff, but laziness pays off now."

"You got that from the Internet," said Mr. Matous, sounding irritated. "I read it on an exchange of one-liners."

He had me there. I *had* gotten it off the Internet. "Lighten up, Mr. Matous. I'm just the class clown. That's why I'm working on a laugh-off."

"I don't think the class clown would be able to pull off a laugh-off. It will require a lot of work."

"My parents didn't think much of your assignment," I said, "especially my father."

"Your parents aren't in my class. You are."

"You're just a first-year teacher," I snapped at Mr. Matous. "You've got to learn sometime."

As soon as the words were out of my mouth, I knew I sounded just like a clone of my father.

"What?" asked Mr. Matous angrily. "What do I have to learn?"

"Some kids are complete goof-offs. You've got to learn that you should just write some kids off."

"Thanks for the advice, Bobby," said Mr. Matous. "But I like your humor much better when it's not sarcastic. Why don't you look up the word 'sarcasm' and define it for me? Consider it an extra-extra homework assignment. Today is

Thursday. I'll give you the weekend. I want a preliminary plan for the laugh-off on my desk by
Monday morning, along with all your other work
and a definition of the word 'sarcasm.' Now get
out of here."

I hesitated. "Mr. Matous . . . I'm sorry."

"So am I," said Mr. Matous.

☺

CHAPTER 11

What kind of jokes did Einstein make?

Wisecracks!

I walked down the stairs and out of school. I squinted in the cold March light. Janeen was leaning on the wall of the school, by a mural that we had painted last year in fourth grade. It showed a row of kids in all the colors of the rainbow. Janeen and I had drawn two figures right next to each other. Janeen's figure looked happy and normal. Mine looked a little demonic, but our two figures were holding hands. In school, the only time you could hold hands was when you were little and being marched down the hall for assemblies or recess. Janeen and I used to hold hands then. But kids our age don't hold hands anymore. Not if they don't want to be teased to death.

When we were making the mural, I told Janeen that I didn't feel like a normal kid, that I felt like everybody else had some secret about how to behave that nobody had taught me. She said she thought everybody felt that way, but that only true friends admitted it to each other.

"Hey, Janeen, thanks for waiting," I said. "You're a true friend."

She looked at me suspiciously. "Is that sarcastic?"

I felt close to tears. "No," I said. "Don't you remember? It was something you said to me when we painted our characters on the mural. You said that everybody feels like they're not normal, but only true friends could say it out loud."

Janeen looked a little proud that I had remembered her words. "I think I got that from a Paul Zindel book," she said. "I'm glad you remembered." I was glad that I had made her happy. I wasn't making too many people happy lately.

"Mr. Matous wants me to put on a real laugh-off as an extra assignment," I told her. "It's the only way I have a chance to stay out of the School for Intervention."

"A real laugh-off?" said Janeen. "What *is* a laugh-off?"

"That's what I've got to figure out. I guess first we'd have the teachers tell us all those things they laugh about in the teachers' room. And then the kids could get up and tell jokes. And then the best kid and the best teacher would have to face off against each other in the laugh-off."

Janeen turned to me. "That sounds fun! And we can invite parents."

"Oh, right," I said, sarcastically. "Maybe I should let my dad take the stage and tell some of his Bobby jokes. 'If space aliens captured Bobby, they'd report no intelligent life on earth.'"

"That's not funny. It's mean," said Janeen. Sometimes I forget that all dads don't sound like mine. I felt a little uncomfortable. "Dad's not one hundred percent mean," I said.

"Nobody's one hundred percent of anything," said Janeen.

"Maybe you could sell that to a fortune-cookie company."

Janeen looked hurt. I dug in my pocket and handed her a quarter. "What's this for?" she asked.

"Your put-down fund," I said. "I always think of my dad as the put-down artist, not me."

"Mostly you make fun of yourself. It's different."

I was a little embarrassed that we were talking about this stuff. I wanted to change the subject. "So will you help me with this laugh-off? You're good at practical stuff."

Janeen looked relieved to change the subject too. "Well, the first thing you've got to do is arrange the auditorium. They schedule assemblies way in advance, so you'll have to get a date from Dr. Deal."

"Go to the principal's office voluntarily? You've got to be out of your mind. I can see it now. Excuse me, Dr. Deal, I know you think I'm so dumb that I flunk recess, but let me have the auditorium so I can have a laugh-off even though there is no such thing."

"There was no Velcro until someone made it up," said Janeen. "There was no karate until someone made it up."

"What's the point?" I asked.

"Somebody makes up all the things that are good. The laugh-off is your invention. So tell me, what are the rules?"

"Rules?"

"It has to have some rules."

I thought about it. "I'm not good at rules. I don't want too many rules."

"How do we judge? Who wins?" asked Janeen.

"The laughing!" I said. "It's the only way. No voting. The person who gets the most laughs wins. I guess I'll have to find a fair person to be the judge and keep track of how many real laughs a person gets and which laugh is the loudest."

"I've got to start thinking of jokes," said

Janeen. "I've got one. I got it from a book. What kind of jokes did Einstein make?"

I looked at her. "Wisecracks."

"It's not that funny, is it?" said Janeen.

"Well, jokes from a book aren't as funny as ones you just think up yourself—what *you* think is funny." I thought about how Mr. Matous had so quickly picked up the line that I had gotten from the Internet.

"Do you think I'm funny?" Janeen asked.

"You're smart, you're loyal and you're a true friend," I said honestly.

"But I'm not funny," said Janeen. I shook my head. I couldn't lie to her.

"Will you help me get funny?" Janeen asked.

"I'll try," I said, "if you'll help me with the laugh-off."

"I will," said Janeen. "Here's another joke: Knock, knock."

I sighed. Janeen loved knock-knock jokes as much as Jimmy and Dad did, but she always got them a little wrong.

"Who's there?" I said.

"Boo hoo," said Janeen. Then she looked stricken. "Whoops! I was supposed to say 'Boo,' then you say 'Boo who?' Then I say 'Why are you crying?'"

"It's okay," I said. "It's a hard joke to ruin."

Janeen looked like she had been insulted. Maybe she had been insulted a little. She glared at me. "I think we may need a few more rules for your laugh-off."

I rolled my eyes. "Not too many rules. Kids will tell their jokes. Teachers will tell theirs. And then at the end, the kid who gets the most laughs will have a final laugh-off against the teacher who gets the most laughs. And the one who gets the biggest laughs wins. That's all the rules I want."

"I bet Dr. Deal will want a few more."

I groaned. I couldn't believe that I was actually going to have to voluntarily see the principal. But there was no way around it.

CHAPTER 12

Why is everybody tired on April Fool's Day?

They just finished a long March.

On Friday, I went into the principal's office. Ms. Lofti looked up when she saw me. "So what are you in for this time, Bobby?" she joked.

"I'm not in trouble. I just wanted to see Dr. Deal."

"You *want* to see Dr. Deal?" asked Ms. Lofti. "And nobody's making you?"

"Actually, I'm never really in trouble. I just keep asking Mr. Matous to send me here so I can see you."

"Bobby, you don't have to flatter me—I can't change your grades. And Dr. Deal is very busy today. I don't think she has time to see you."

"Can't you just sneak me in?" I asked. "Everybody knows that you're the real power around here."

"Bobby, you're terrible. Have a cookie, and I'll see what I can do."

Just then Dr. Deal came out of her office with a computer printout that she gave to Ms. Lofti. She looked at me and made a little face. I guess I just bring that out in principals.

"I'm not in trouble," I said quickly. "Honest. I just need to talk to you about an extra project that Mr. Matous wants me to do."

"Dr. Deal," interrupted Ms. Lofti, "the reading consultant called just a minute ago. She'll be fifteen minutes late."

Dr. Deal sighed. "All right, Bobby, come in."

As I walked into Dr. Deal's office's, Ms. Lofti winked at me. I knew the phone hadn't rung in the past few minutes. I had a feeling that Ms. Lofti was willing to make the reading consultant wait. I'd have to remember to thank her.

Dr. Deal shut the door behind her. "Okay, Bobby, what is it? I don't have much time."

I took a deep breath. When people tell you they don't have much time, it makes it hard to talk. "I want to hold a school-wide laugh-off, and I'll need the auditorium," I blurted out.

"A what?" demanded Dr. Deal. "What's a laugh-off."

"Well, you see, a lot of people are asking that question, Dr. Deal. Is it just a joke contest? No.

Not just a joke contest. Everybody knows that the teachers tell funny stories when we're not around—and kids tell funny stories when the teachers aren't around. So this will be a contest— a laugh-off—between the teachers and the kids to see who's funniest."

"Whose idea was this?" asked Dr. Deal suspiciously.

"Uh, mine."

"This isn't an early April Fool's joke, is it?"

I practically jumped out of my chair. "What a great idea!" I exploded. "Can we have it on April Fool's Day? That would be terrific. By the way, do you know why everybody's tired on April Fool's day?"

"No," said Dr. Deal. She sounded a little leery.

"Because they just finished a long March. Get it? The month of March is long. Thirty-one days, and it's cold and miserable."

"I get it, Bobby," said Dr. Deal. "Have you ever attended a laugh-off?" she asked.

"Uh, I don't think there's ever been one."

"I see," said Dr. Deal. "And you plan to hold the very first one in our school? And who is going to do all the planning and work?"

"Me," I said. "Well, you did tell Mr. Matous to give me extra assignments. This is what he came up with."

I was nervous. I kept drumming my fingers on the edge of the chair.

"Please stop that," said Dr. Deal. I stopped. I couldn't read the expression on her face.

"I think it would do a lot for school spirit," I rattled on. I didn't even know why I was trying so hard. I should have known that Dr. Deal would shoot my idea down. I might as well face it—I'd be going to the School for Intervention anyhow.

Dr. Deal leaned back in her chair. She stared at the ceiling. "Did you hear about the kindergartner who came home from school and told her parents that she wasn't going back?" she asked.

"No." I wondered what the laugh-off had to do with a kid in kindergarten.

"The little girl's parents asked her why she didn't want to go back to school. 'Did something bad happen?' they asked.

"'No,' the little girl said. 'But the principal told us she wanted us to have school spirit, and I'm not going to any school that's haunted.'" Dr. Deal laughed.

I stared at Dr. Deal. "That was a joke," I said.

"Yes, of course it was. I love jokes. I think of myself as a very funny person. Now, let me look at the schedule. April Fool's Day. That's in just three weeks. Do you think that will give you enough time?"

"Janeen offered to help me," I said. "We can get some other kids to help. But I've got to find a judge. I figure the person who gets the loudest laughs wins, but there should be a judge in case it's not so easy to tell."

I was hoping that Dr. Deal wouldn't insist on being the judge. I knew there was no way I would win if she were the judge. "You know, Ms. Lofti might be a good judge," she said. "She's very fair and she laughs at my jokes."

Dr. Deal turned to her computer and studied the school calendar. "I think a laugh-off on April Fool's Day would be very appropriate. The auditorium is available during first period. That's always a good time to have school-wide events. Everybody is fresh."

I couldn't believe what I was hearing. There was actually going to be a laugh-off. Wait until I told Janeen! Wait until I told Mr. Matous!

"Now I think we should go over rules and regulations," said Dr. Deal.

"Rules and regulations?" I asked, feeling my stomach sink.

"Yes," said Dr. Deal. "Rules may be an alien concept to you, but the contest should have rules."

I didn't appreciate her sarcasm, and I was glad that Janeen had already brought up the subject. "Uh, I think the only rule should be that all contestants try to be funny," I said. "And no one gets more than three minutes. I watch a lot of comics on TV, and believe me, three minutes can seem like a very long time."

"That sounds fine," said Dr. Deal. "I like the amount of preliminary thought that you've put into this. I think we should have some guidelines for the kinds of jokes that can be told. There will be no dirty jokes. No cruel jokes. No bathroom jokes."

"How about no jokes?"

Dr. Deal laughed. "Bobby, you are funny. However, there are plenty of jokes that you can make using those guidelines. Oh, and put me down as one of the contestants."

I stared at her. Somehow I had never imagined Dr. Deal in the laugh-off. When would I put her on? It was a little like the joke about where you put an eight-hundred-pound gorilla—anywhere she wants.

"Keep me posted," said Dr. Deal. "I want to know how you're progressing."

"Thanks, Dr. Deal. I never thought you'd say yes."

"You never know until you ask," said Dr.

Deal. "That's a good lesson in life. Maybe I'll use that as my thought for the day." I started to leave. "Bobby," said Dr. Deal. I turned back.

"I want you to think about something. If you hadn't dug such a deep hole for yourself by not doing your homework and acting out all year, this would have been easier. I want you to know that I'm still watching you. This laugh-off is not an excuse for not doing the rest of your work."

"Yes, Dr. Deal."

She was looking at me strangely. I had the feeling that I should make my getaway as quickly as possible.

"I want your conscience to guide you. Do you want to hear one of my favorite jokes?"

When a principal asks a question like that, there's only one answer.

"Uh, y-yes," I stammered.

"A conscience is a bothersome thing. It lets us know when we've done wrong and will not let us rest until we've set things right. No wonder so many people try to kill it early on. Bobby, I don't want you to kill your conscience."

That was a joke?! I had entered the twilight zone. I didn't have the slightest idea what she was talking about. I wasn't worried about Dr. Deal winning the laugh-off. If that was her idea of a good joke, she was going to bomb. But I had

other things to worry about. I had to try to organize a school-wide laugh-off in exactly three
weeks. I didn't think I could do that and worry
about my conscience too.

CHAPTER 13

Knock, knock.

Who's there?

Dummy.

Dummy Who?

Dummy a favor and get lost!

Maybe Dr. Deal's thing about the conscience had actually worked on me. Suddenly I seemed to be developing one about doing my homework. Over the weekend, I did almost all of mine. I also made a preliminary plan for the laugh-off to hand in to Mr. Matous. I was feeling kind of smug when late on Sunday afternoon, I remembered that Mr. Matous had asked me to look up "sarcasm." Grandma and Mom had gone out to a movie, one that Dad hadn't wanted to see.

Dad was doing some work at his desk in the living room. My parents have a big dictionary, one that my father is proud of. The print is so small that it comes with its own magnifying glass. I went into the living room to use it. Dad ignored me, even though I knew he had seen me come in. I looked up "sarcasm." The dictionary defined it as the use of "biting gibes and taunting language." I copied the words down in my notebook. It sounded awful written down like that, somehow much worse than just the word "sarcasm." The dictionary said the word came from a Greek word meaning "to tear flesh, to bite the lips in rage." I stared off into space. I chewed on my pencil.

Dad must have sensed me thinking about him. He looked up from his work. "What are you doing?" Dad asked. "You look tired. Have you been thinking?"

"Thanks for the example of sarcasm," I said to him. "Part of my homework was to look up the word. It's very nasty."

"Nasty?" repeated Dad. "I think it shows intelligence and wit. People know you're teasing when you're sarcastic. It's for people who grow out of knock-knock jokes."

"Jimmy and I loved it when you taught us knock-knock jokes. Remember 'Car go beep, beep'"? Jimmy and I were just laughing about that joke. You know, Jimmy, my brother. Your other son."

"That's a fine example of sarcasm," said Dad

dryly. He blinked. I wondered if he was remembering all the times the three of us traded jokes. I wondered if there was a part of him that missed Jimmy too. "There's nothing wrong with knock-knock jokes," he admitted. "I just think you outgrow them."

"Janeen still loves them."

"Well, Janeen is a nice girl, but she's not exactly the sharpest tack in the box."

"Janeen is one of the smartest kids in the class, Dad. She's no dummy."

"Then what's she doing hanging around with you?" teased Dad. He must have read something in my face. "Hey, I was only kidding," he said quickly.

"Knock, knock," I said.

"Who's there?" asked Dad.

"Dummy."

"Dummy who?" asked Dad, playing along.

"Dummy a favor and get lost."

Dad looked at me. "Is that a joke you're planning on using in your laugh-off?"

"I haven't decided," I said. "My books on comedy say that you should come up with an attitude. I don't want mine to be sarcastic, especially now that I know it means 'to tear flesh.'"

"'Tear flesh'?" repeated Dad.

"Yes, that's what it really means," I said.

"Let me see your homework. I'll check it for you."

I froze for a second. I didn't want to hand my homework to my father.

"Give it to me. I told Mr. Matous that I'd check your homework."

I remembered that he had. Reluctantly I handed him the piece of paper. "You copied this straight out of the dictionary and you still misspelled half the words. And your writing is like chicken scratches—what does this say?"

I looked over his shoulder. My mouth was close to his neck. "It says 'sarcastic' comes from a Greek word meaning 'to tear flesh or bite the lips in rage.'"

I moved slightly away from him. It's not that I really thought I was going to bite him like a vampire. The thought flashed through my mind that the only way to kill a vampire was to put a stake through his heart.

Dad swung his chair around. He handed me back my homework. "I think you should do it over," he said. "If it's worth doing, it's worth doing right."

"I'm not a perfectionist like you," I said.

"A perfectionist is not such a terrible thing. It's someone who's willing to take infinite pains to get something right."

"Right," I said. "And gives infinite pains to everyone around him."

"That's very funny, Bobby, but I keep telling you there's such a thing as being too funny," warned Dad.

"Great advice to a kid who's about to organize a laugh-off," I said. I took my homework back from him.

Dad leaned back. "I wasn't too impressed with your teacher. He seemed awfully young. And this laugh-off idea is silly. Now, looking up words like 'sarcasm'—at least you're learning something."

"We learn a lot. Mr. Matous is a good teacher. Janeen thinks he's terrific, and so do her parents."

"Anything Janeen and her family think is A-okay with you."

"Janeen gets very good grades."

"Mm-hmm. I think you have a little crush on Janeen."

"Don't tease me about Janeen. We've been friends forever. She's helping me with the laugh-off."

"I wish I knew what your teacher hoped to accomplish with this laugh-off."

"He thinks I'm funny. Is that such a problem?"

"I don't have a problem with it. I think you got your sense of humor from me."

I stared at him. "You! You're the master of the put-down. That's not me."

"Master of the put-down," repeated my father. I couldn't tell if he thought it was a compliment or an insult. "I don't put you down. I just tell you the truth. Some of your friends only tell you the nice things about yourself, but they lie. I tell you the truth."

"Does that mean there are no nice things to say about me?" I demanded.

My father looked away. "That's your interpretation," he said quietly. I thought he was being sarcastic, but I couldn't tell. I folded my piece of paper with its definition of "sarcasm," and I went into my room to check over the rest of my homework. I took down some of my comedy books and tried to think of what my attitude should be for the laugh-off. One of my favorite books, *Stand-up Comedy: The Book*, by Judy Carter, says that you should always start by making fun of yourself: "*Is there something about your personality that you don't like?*"

Okay, I made a list.

1. My put-downs are so mean, my parents ran away from home. (I liked that one—even if it wasn't true.)

2. I'm so dumb, I once put a rubber band around

my head to stretch my mind.

3. I'm so dumb, my father thinks the nearest I've ever come to a brainstorm is a light drizzle.

4. My father once made me look up "empty" in a dictionary. Boy, was I surprised to see a picture of my head pasted in there.

Now that, I thought, was funny.

CHAPTER 14

What do you do when your nose goes on strike?

Picket.

I got to class a little early on Monday. I went up to Mr. Matous's desk and gave him my extra homework—the definition of "sarcasm." Mr. Matous read it and then looked up at me. "Bobby, this is excellent work. I loved the way you put in the Greek origin of the word. I didn't know that. It's fascinating. It tells us that the word always meant something that hurts. Like someone biting you—hard! This is terrific. Do you understand why I don't like sarcasm?"

"Yeah, I guess so, because it's mean."

"Exactly. It's almost always directed at somebody else. I've always thought the funniest people tell jokes on themselves."

"So you really *mean* I did okay? The spelling wasn't crummy?"

Mr. Matous smiled. "You just made a pun—on the word 'mean.' That was very clever. You did misspell a couple of words"—he got out his red pen—"here and here, but this was a great effort. Keep up the good work."

I kind of bounced back to my desk. I don't often hear words like "great effort, good work." They have their own kind of cool sound to them. And the good feeling lasted most of the day.

I had made plans with Janeen to work on some of the details for the laugh-off after school. "We've got a lot to do," I reminded her as we walked down the steps of school. "The date is less than three weeks away. Dr. Deal will kill me if I screw up."

Unfortunately, Willie overheard us. "A date. I knew you two were dating. I just didn't know you needed permission from the principal. Hoo-hah."

"We're not dating, you jerk!" said Janeen.

I was glad she called Willie a jerk, but she didn't have to sound like a date with me would be like going out with a lower life form.

"Willie," I said, remembering a joke that Jimmy had told me, "I heard you almost had a date once, but she chewed off her leg and escaped."

"You both are disgusting," said Janeen. "I hope you're aren't going to let jokes like that in the laugh-off."

"What laugh-off?" asked Willie. "That thing you talked about in class, between the teachers and the kids?"

I nodded. "We're actually going to have one—on April Fool's Day. It'll be a joke contest between the teachers and the kids."

"Cool," said Willie. "I'll enter. I've got a ton of jokes. What do you do when your nose goes on strike?"

"I don't know," said Janeen.

"Picket." Willie laughed as if it were the funniest joke he had ever heard.

"Isn't there a rule against jokes that make you gag?" asked Janeen.

"No," I said. "Dr. Deal didn't say anything about yucky jokes, and I refuse to keep them out! After all, it's supposed to be about jokes that make *us* laugh."

"You mean we have to tell these jokes in front of her?" Willie exclaimed.

"That's the point," I said. "It's our chance to hear what teachers are always laughing about and never tell us, and they'll hear our jokes. Then the funniest kid and the funniest teacher face off against each other. Whoever gets the most laughs wins."

I couldn't believe how real the laugh-off had begun to seem.

"I've got another one," said Willie. "It's not

dirty. Just disgusting. What's the difference between boogers and broccoli?"

Janeen shrugged her shoulders. "I don't know."

"Kids don't eat broccoli," said Willie.

I laughed. "That's pretty funny."

"Hey Bobby," said Willie. "Look's who's waiting for you." I looked across the street. Jimmy was leaning against the wall, smoking a cigar. He took a big drag, then exhaled, letting out a stream of smoke.

Janeen and I walked across the street. Jimmy held out his hand for a high five. "Aren't you glad to see me? Hi, Janeen."

Janeen held her nose. "That cigar stinks," she whispered to me.

I slapped Jimmy's palm. "I'm glad to see you," I said. "I just wasn't expecting you."

"Well, I was just thinking about my little brother. I knew you'd be getting out of school. Excuse us, Janeen. I've got an idea I want to talk to Bobby about."

"Bobby and I have to design the fliers for the laugh-off on my computer," said Janeen.

"What's a laugh-off?" Jimmy asked.

"It's Bobby's idea," said Janeen. "It's a joke contest. And the whole school is going to be involved."

"That's my brother—the comedian," Jimmy

said. He sounded proud. He blew a little cigar smoke my way.

I tried to wave the smoke away. "That does stink," I said. Janeen nodded her head.

"You just don't know quality," said Jimmy.

"Yeah, well, your cigar smells like a cross between a bear and a skunk," I said.

"What's that?" asked Jimmy.

"Winnie the P.U."

Jimmy laughed. He always laughs at my jokes. He put his arm around my shoulder. "Come on, little bro."

I shrugged at Janeen. "We'll do the fliers on the school computer tomorrow," I said. She looked disappointed. Jimmy kept his arm around me and guided me to a stoop around the corner.

"A laugh-off," said Jimmy. "I've got some jokes for you if you want. You can buy them from me. Don't comedians buy jokes?"

"Buy jokes? Who do you think I am, Richie Rich?"

"I've got a joke for you for free. When our dad was born, they passed out cigars. When I was born, they passed out cigarettes. When you were born—they just passed out."

"Thanks, I think I'll pass on that joke."

"Here's another one for free. Why do farts smell?"

"Uh, Jimmy, I don't think the principal wants any fart jokes."

"So deaf people don't miss all the fun," said Jimmy.

I groaned. "A giant pass on that one," I said.

Jimmy gave me a low five. "Well, I've got a million other jokes. But the next one you'll have to buy. I'm a little short right now. How are you for cash?"

"Me? *I'm* a little short. You might have noticed I'm your little brother. I'm just a kid. You're the big brother. All I've got is my allowance, and that's not much."

"Yeah, but you're a smart little kid. I know you. I bet you've got some money stashed away. I've got an idea. You give me what you've got stashed, and I'll take you to a poker game. We'll both make some money. You remember what I taught you about playing poker?"

Mostly what Jimmy had taught me was how to cheat, or more exactly how to help Jimmy cheat. He taught me an elaborate set of signals so that I could tell him what was in Dad's hand when we played poker with Grandma and some of my aunts and uncles and cousins. It's kind of a family tradition to play poker on holidays and summer vacations. It made Dad furious to lose to Jimmy, and I always thought it was kind of fun to help Jimmy cheat. But not that much fun. I never got to win, only Jimmy.

"I'll tell you what," said Jimmy. "Tomorrow, cut school. I can get you into a poker game. I'll tell the guys you're like a little idiot savant. You know what that is?"

"No, but I don't like the idea of anybody calling me an idiot."

"It means an idiot who's very good at something," said Jimmy. "So here's what we're going to do. You'll skip school. I'll bring you to the game. We can clean up." Jimmy rubbed his hands together. "It'll be great."

"Jimmy, I can't skip school," I told him. "I'm on probation. They'll send me to the School for Intervention. My teacher is giving me a second chance, and so is the principal. But it all depends on the laugh-off."

"Don't tell me you've been begging them to let you stay in school? You shouldn't beg for anything."

What a lousy rule. Jimmy was afraid to beg to be allowed to come back home, and Mom and Dad were afraid to beg him to come home. It was a standoff, like some gunfight in an old Western.

"I didn't beg," I protested. "My teacher *wanted* to give me a second chance. But I will beg you. Don't ask me to skip school."

Jimmy took a puff of his cigar. He blew smoke in my face.

"Thanks," I said sarcastically. I waved the smoke away. "Will you come to my laugh-off? You and Grandma are the only ones in the family who ever laugh at my jokes, especially lately. I need you there."

Jimmy looked at me. He grinned. I love Jimmy's smile. "I'll be there," he said.

"Promise?"

"Will Mom and Dad be there?" he asked.

I sighed. "I don't know. Probably, but it's a big auditorium."

"I'll be there for you, kid," said Jimmy. Then he started to walk away.

"Jimmy, wait!" I said. "If you really need money, you should tell Mom and Dad. They would help."

"I don't need anybody's help," he said. He walked off, looking cocky, but I knew that I had let him down.

CHAPTER 15

Knock, knock.

Who's there?

Noah.

Noah Who?

Noah body. April Fool!

Janeen had decided that we had to start calling it the Great Laugh-Off. "It's such a great idea," she said. I have to admit that I loved hearing it called that. We designed our fliers.

SO JUST HOW FUNNY ARE YOU?

FIND OUT! SIGN UP!

ENTER THE GREAT LAUGH-OFF!

KIDS VS. TEACHERS

APRIL FOOL'S DAY—NO FOOLING!

We were in the computer lab when Mr. Weinstein, the computer teacher, came over and picked up one of our fliers. "I've been hearing about the laugh-off. It sounds like fun."

"Thanks," I said. "Things are really rolling along. Everyone is helping. We got the pizza parlor to donate gift certificates to the runners-up. Mr. Matous says that he's taking care of the trophy for the winner. He says he's getting a store to donate a special trophy since this is the first official laugh-off."

"So what do you have to do if you want to be in it?" asked Mr. Weinstein.

I handed him a sheet. "Here's a list of the rules. Dr. Deal looked it over and said it was okay. No dirty jokes. If someone tells a dirty joke, Ms. Lofti will ring a bell and the person will have to leave the stage immediately and be disqualified."

"I'm impressed," said Mr. Weinstein. "You've really worked this out."

I noticed that the computer was taking a long time to print out our fliers. "Did I do something wrong?" I asked him.

"Naw, these computers are just ancient," said Mr. Weinstein. "They're so old, they came with an abacus as a backup. Get it? That's an ancient Chinese calculator. That's a good joke—maybe I'll use it in the laugh-off."

I didn't have the heart to tell Mr. Weinstein

that his joke wasn't that funny. Lately a lot of people had been telling me bad jokes.

Janeen and I put the fliers up all over school. Kids kept stopping me and telling me what a great idea they thought it was. "I've started to practice my jokes," said Janeen. "I want to surprise people."

"Not everybody has to be funny," I said.

"Thank you very much," said Janeen. "I'll have you know that I can be anything I want to be. I have a lot of willpower."

"I'm not sure willpower can help you be funny."

Janeen gave me a dirty look. "I've made a list of jokes that I'm going to tell." Janeen took out her list.

"Do you ever not have a list?"

"Is that supposed to be funny?" asked Janeen.

Those weren't my favorite words. I shook my head. "No; sorry."

"Give me some pointers! I'm going to start with a joke about the auditorium."

"Janeen, just tell the joke. You don't have to give it a big setup. That's one of the things my books tell me. Keep working at making your jokes shorter."

Janeen took out her notebook and wrote something down.

"What are you writing?"

"To remember to make my jokes shorter."

"That's not something you could just remember without writing it down?"

Janeen made a face. "Okay, this is my first joke. See, it's about the auditorium. Oh, oops, I wasn't going to say that. It's a good thing we're not having the laugh-off in the mushroom," said Janeen.

I stared at her. "What?"

"Because the mushroom is the one room you can't go into. Wasn't that funny? Mushrooms aren't really a room—so that means it's a room that you can't go into."

"Hmm. Maybe if you make fun of the fact that it's such a bad joke. Use it as a callback."

"What's that?"

"You remind the audience of a bad joke that you made—or call back something that was funny before."

"Okay, I get it—sort of," said Janeen.

"Why don't you tell me your other jokes?"

"Okay, this one is great, because it's about April Fool's Day and we're having the laugh-off on April Fool's Day." Janeen put her hand to her mouth. "I told the punchline."

"Just go ahead," I said as gently as I could.

"Knock, knock."

"Who's there?" I said.

"Noah."

"Noah who?"

"Noah body—April Fool!"

Janeen waited. "Don't you think that's brilliant? See, we're having the laugh-off on April Fool's Day."

"I got it," I said.

"Okay, here's another one. What would you get if you crossed a pigeon, a frog and a prehistoric monster?"

"What?"

"You'd get a pigeon-toed dinosaur. Get it? A pigeon, and a frog is a toad, and a dinosaur is a prehistoric monster. It's a pun *and* a riddle."

"Yeah, I get it, Janeen, but it's not really all that funny. See, there's more to being funny than just telling jokes."

"I thought my pigeon-toed joke was funny," said Janeen defensively. "And the knock-knock joke was brilliant."

"Maybe your attitude should be that you can't tell a joke. Then you could get the audience on your side."

"Tell me how," insisted Janeen.

"No one can really tell you how to do it. You have to find something that you think is funny and then exaggerate it. Or make fun of something that you already do. Like you could make fun of the fact that you're so organized. I bet the first thing on your list is 'Make a list.'"

"I don't understand why that's funny." Janeen looked worried. "Let me try again. Knock, knock."

"Who's there?" I said.

"Boo."

I stopped her. "Janeen, I wouldn't do that joke. Kids tell that joke in kindergarten."

Janeen got a stubborn look around her jaw. "You're supposed to say, 'Boo who?' and I say, 'Don't cry.'"

"Janeen, don't you see? The only way that joke will be funny is if you make fun of it. I mean, it's such an old joke. That joke is so corny, it could feed a chicken for five years."

"Stop being so critical," said Janeen, sounding frustrated. She flung the remaining fliers at me. "You do all the work yourself, if you're so darned funny!"

"Janeen, come back!" I shouted.

Mr. Matous came around the corner. "What's wrong with Janeen?" he asked. "I just saw her running down the hall. She looked upset."

"I can't figure it out. She asked me to help her be funny, and then when I tried, she got mad at me."

Mr. Matous started to laugh.

"What's so funny about Janeen being mad at me?"

"Nothing," said Mr. Matous. "It's just that that's the way I feel every day when I'm teaching. Sometimes the most frustrating things are the most funny. Did you ever notice that really funny comics aren't perfect? It's much more interesting to watch someone who's got problems."

"Then I must be one funny guy."

"You are," said Mr. Matous. He patted me on the shoulder. "I'm impressed with what you've done so far to get the laugh-off off the ground."

I couldn't believe it. First Mr. Weinstein and now Mr. Matous—the second teacher in one day to be impressed with me. This had to be one for the *Guinness Book of Records*.

CHAPTER 16

Knock, knock.

Who's there?

Howard.

Howard Who?

How hard can it be to guess a knock-knock joke is coming!

The Great Laugh-Off was only one week away. I was running around like a chicken without a head. I had to go to the pizza parlor to collect the gift certificates for all the runners-up. I had to update my computer list of all the contestants and decide in what order they should go on. We had lots of contestants, more than enough to fill the time we had. Ms. Lofti had agreed to be the judge. Mr. Weinstein had printed out a program.

I hardly had time to work on my own routine. I knew everybody expected me to blow them away with my jokes. I had a partial plan. I had a joke about the head lice. I had a couple of jokes about being the class clown. I had jokes about Dad thinking I was dumb. But none of it pulled together.

I stood in front of the mirror. One of my books said to practice in front of a mirror, but I felt like such a geek. My ears stuck out. Maybe looking funny was a blessing.

"Knock, knock," said a voice behind me.

I turned. Grandma was standing in back of me with a load of clean clothes in her arms.

"Who's there?" I asked.

"Howard," she said.

"Howard who?"

"How hard can it be to guess a knock-knock joke is coming?" we said together.

"Did you teach that joke to Dad?" I asked her.

She shook her head. "I think your father taught it to me." She put my laundry on the bed and sat down. "So are you ready for the Great Laugh-Off?"

I shook my head. "I'm worried. I can make kids laugh in class, but can I really do it onstage? I haven't had much time to practice. Some books say that you shouldn't rehearse too much."

"Stop worrying so much. Practice on me. I can be your audience."

"Uh, I don't know, Grandma." I paused. "Grandma, would you be mad at me if I told a joke about you thinking my head lice were doing the jitterbug?"

"Would it get a laugh?" Grandma asked.

"I think so."

"Use it!" said Grandma. "Okay, slay me." She crossed her arms over her chest. "Isn't that what comedians try to do?" she asked.

I nodded. My mouth felt dry.

"Hi, everybody. I'm so dumb, my father thinks the nearest I've ever come to a brainstorm is a light drizzle."

Grandma frowned. "I don't think that's so funny," she said.

I thought a minute. "Okay," I said. "How about this? Hi, everybody. I tried not to do knock-knock jokes, but you know what? The knock-knock monster came. It was a she. She went knock, knock . . ."

I paused. "See, I figure everybody will say, 'Who's there?' It'll involve the audience."

"Okay," said Grandma, but she looked a little doubtful. So was I. I had made fun of Janeen for using knock-knock jokes, and here they were, right at the center of my routine. "Who's there?" said Grandma.

"Lucretia."

"Lucretia who?" asked Grandma.

"Lucretia from the Black Lagoon!" I shouted out.

At least that got a groan from Grandma.

"Sorry, folks, I can't help myself," I said. When I was making fun of myself, I could feel myself relax. I glanced down at my notes.

"What is gray, sits on buildings and is very dangerous?"

"I don't know," said Grandma.

"A pigeon with a machine gun."

Grandma held up her hand. "Wait a minute, honey. The jokes are funny, but you need a little more attitude. Don't just tell one joke after another. Let the audience know who you are. You're not just a joke machine. You're the kid who gets into trouble because he's so funny that he can't stop himself. He always wants to entertain. Exaggerate that, and the audience will love you."

I stared at her. "Grandma, that's exactly what all the books say. But when I told you the joke about how dumb I was, you didn't seem to like it. See, all my books say you've got to have a gimmick—a shtick—and I thought mine should be: I'm so dumb—"

"You're not dumb," protested Grandma. "That's not who you are, my sweet, smart boy. Your dad's got the smarts, too, but somehow he's forgotten about the sweetness. No, your job is to let people see you for who you are. That's what's going to make this comedy routine sing. Anybody can tell jokes."

"That's what I told Janeen, but I'm really scared that I don't have it. I am not exactly sure how to bring it out."

"So you practice with me, and I'll help you bring it out. Now, come on. Let's punch up your jokes."

"I'm the kid who gets in trouble in school," I said, trying to get into my routine. "Everybody knows it. But it's not my fault. I mean I just try to answer the questions. In geography my teacher asked me, 'What can you tell me about the Dead Sea?' 'Gee,' I said, 'I didn't even know it was sick.'"

Grandma laughed. "Much better," she said. "But I still think we need to see more of you."

I scratched my ear. "What do you think I should make jokes about?"

Grandma shrugged. "I think it has to come from what you think is important. Like what do you want to be when you grow up?"

"If you ask Dad, he'll tell you I should consider a career as a crash dummy."

"That's sick. Did your dad really say that to you?"

"No," I admitted. "I made that one up, but I just know that's what he thinks. Dad's not worried that I'll have a mental breakdown. He doesn't believe I've got any moving parts up here." I pointed to my head.

Grandma winced. "Ouch! That hurts," she said.

I thought about all the hours she and I had spent watching comics and all the books that I had about comedy. They all said the same thing: All the material you'll ever need is inside you. And the more it hurts, the funnier it can be.

I took out my notebook. "Grandma," I said. "I think I want to be alone. I want to write some new stuff."

"Good," said Grandma. One reason I love her is that she doesn't ask too many questions.

I sat down at my computer, and I started thinking about Jimmy and me and Dad. Some of what I wrote cut a little too close to the bone. I didn't know if I'd have the nerve to say some of these things out loud. When a joke doesn't go over, comics say they died. I could die up there in front of the mike, in front of everybody. I really could. But I kept writing.

CHAPTER 17

☺
+ +

What is a witch doctor's mistake?

A Voodoo boo-boo.

We held a rehearsal for the Great Laugh-Off after school on March 30. We had less than two days to pull the whole thing together. In addition to doing my own routine, Janeen had insisted that I was the only one who could be MC. That means the master of ceremonies. I had to introduce everybody. Master of Disaster was more like it.

Most of the kids didn't know how to talk into the microphone. I kept telling them to talk louder. The audience needed to be able to hear their jokes. My comedy books talked about "getting intimate with the microphone." Everybody giggled as if I were saying something dirty, but that's not what it meant. It meant that they had to talk with the microphone right up to their lips. If you watch singers on MTV, you'll notice they always hold the mike way up close to their mouths. Most of the kids and even the teachers acted as if they thought the microphone would give them poison ivy.

And a lot of the jokes were terrible. Some of the teachers told worse jokes than the kids did. A lot of them hadn't bothered to work up a routine at all. Some of them seemed afraid to tell us what they laughed about in the teachers' room. They told jokes so old that if Adam came back to life, he'd recognize them.

Ms. Krosnick, the fourth-grade teacher, asked, "Why did the timid doctor tiptoe past the medicine cabinet?" She muttered the punch line: "He didn't want to wake up the sleeping pills."

Then Ms. Siscoe, the second-grade teacher, asked what you got if you crossed a Boy Scout with a kangaroo. "A kangaroo that helps old ladies hop across the street." She giggled. At least she was enjoying herself.

The next teacher's joke was just as bad. "What is a witch doctor's mistake?" asked Ms. Lorenzo. "A voodoo boo-boo!" She waited as if she expected it to get a big laugh. I didn't think it would.

My favorite little kid at rehearsal was a boy named Zachary. "Knock, knock," said Zach so softly that I couldn't hear him—and I was sitting in the front row.

"Louder," I shouted to him. "Let the audience hear your jokes. Say, *Knock, Knock*!" I yelled it as loud as I could.

"Who's there?" Zach answered.

I started to laugh.

"What did I say that was funny?" he asked.

"I just wanted you to say, 'Knock, knock' louder."

"Oh," said Zach. "So who's there?"

"Who's on first?" I asked.

"What's on second," said Mr. Matous from the back of the auditorium. I turned around. I should have known that he would know that Abbott and Costello routine.

"Okay," I said to Zach. "Let's start from the top. Tell your joke."

"Oswald," said Zach. I stared at him. Then I realized that he was still in the middle of his knock-knock joke and he was too terrified to start over.

"I swallowed my chewing gum," I said. I just wanted to give Zach the punch line so he would know to start over. But Zach started to cry—not little tears. He was really bawling. I stared at him. "What's wrong?"

"That's my joke!" he wailed.

"I know," I said. "I wasn't going to steal it. I'd just heard it before. I was just trying to help."

Mr. Matous came and sat in the auditorium seat next to me. "I think you need to be a little more gentle with some of the little ones. And with some of the big ones too. The teachers all sound really nervous."

"But it's terrible," I said. "You can't hear half the jokes, and the ones that you can hear are awful."

"I thought the kangaroo joke was kind of funny," said Mr. Matous. "You've got to relax."

"How can I relax? I've got to MC the show. Then I've got to do my routine. Then . . ."

"Bobby, it's just a laugh-off. It's supposed to be fun."

"Fun?" I groaned. "Dying's easy. Comedy's hard."

Mr. Matous laughed. "Where did you hear that?"

"In one of my books. An old actor was dying and his agent came to see him. The agent said, 'This must be so hard on you.' The actor looked up and said with his last breath, 'Dying's easy. Comedy is hard.'"

I got out of my seat and went onstage. I knelt down so that my eyes would be on the same level as Zach's. Snot was coming out of his nose. "Say, your nose is running. Don't you think you should chase it?" I asked him.

At least he laughed. I took him backstage and got him a tissue. "Every great comic has bombed at some point," I said. "Bombing is what comics call it when they try to tell a joke and nobody laughs."

Zachary blew his nose.

"And you're lucky," I continued. "It happened at rehearsal. It doesn't count. Now you can go out and do it again."

"I can?" he asked.

"Sure," I said. I led him out to the microphone. I showed him how to hold it close to his mouth.

I sat back down next to Mr. Matous. Zach was much better this time. I gave him a big thumbs-up sign.

"Everyone's excited," said Mr. Matous. "This is going to be really fun."

"Fun?" I groaned. "I've never worked so hard in my life. You probably think it would have been fun to have first-class tickets on the *Titanic*."

"With you, Bobby, even a ride on the *Titanic* would be fun."

Willie's little sister, Emma, was the next one to rehearse. She's only in first grade. Her joke was: "What is the difference between a train and a teacher?"

She grinned out at the auditorium as if she

had just asked the funniest question. "A train goes 'Choo-choo,' but a teacher tells you to take the gum out of your mouth," she shouted out. It was a true groaner, and she told it so fast that you could hardly understand it.

Mr. Matous and I looked at each other. "Dying's easy!" we both said at the same moment. I got out of my chair and went up onto the stage to Emma.

"It's a funny joke," I said to her. "But you have to say it slower. Do you want to try again?"

"I want to get a laugh," Emma said.

"How old are you, Emma?" I asked her.

"Seven," she said.

"Well, it's great that you know that you want to get a laugh." I smiled at her. "I once read in a book that all really good comics knew when they were little that they wanted to make people laugh. So you must be a truly good comic."

She looked up at me as if I had given her the best present on earth. Maybe I had. I had said something nice to her.

CHAPTER 18

How dumb is he?

He thinks noodle soup is brain food.

The long March was almost over. March 31. The afternoon before the Great Laugh-Off. I had worked at shortening my routine and making it snappier. I was trying it out one last time in front of Grandma. Mom and Dad walked in earlier than I had expected them. I stopped immediately. "Go on," said Dad.

I shook my head. "Naw," I said, folding my routine and putting it away. "I don't want to over-rehearse."

"But you rehearse with Grandma. Why not with us?"

I shrugged.

"I like to laugh," said Dad. "Do your routine for me, and we'll see if I find it funny."

"Leave him alone," said Grandma. "Bobby's been working hard. He's got a lot on his mind. He not only has to do his own routine, he's also the master of ceremonies. He's got a very full plate. Tomorrow is going to be a wonderful day."

"No, it's not," I said quickly. "Don't expect too much. At rehearsal, you couldn't hear half the jokes. And even a lot of the teachers were really bad."

"I wish I could have gotten good grades for telling jokes," said Dad. "It would have made school very easy."

"This hasn't been easy," I protested. "You've got no idea how hard I've been working. Mr. Matous and a lot of the teachers have been telling me how impressed they are."

"They must be very impressionable," said Dad.

Grandma stared at Dad. "How could you say that to him!" she demanded.

"Grandma," said Mom, "I'm sure Bobby knew his father was just kidding."

"Gee, Mom, do you want to say that one more time?" I muttered. "I don't think I've ever heard that before."

Mom looked hurt. My father looked a little guilty. "You knew I was kidding, didn't you, Bobby? You know I'm just trying to be funny."

I glared at him. I was sick of his put-downs. "Trying to be funny, Dad, is not the same as being funny," I said in a low voice. "You're not funny. Mom's always telling me that you don't mean what you say. Well, she got the right word at least. You don't *mean* what you say—but it's *mean.* That's a pun! A pun from your son who's so dumb that he thinks noodle soup is brain food! That's part of my routine, Dad. 'My dad thinks I'm so dumb that I think noodle soup is brain food.'"

"You really don't think I'm funny?" Dad asked, ignoring everything else I said, as if that were the most shocking thing I could have said to him.

"No, Dad. You're not funny!" I yelled. "You come into a room and all the air gets sucked out. You can't laugh when you can't breathe!"

"Bobby!" said my mother. I was sick of her too. I went to my room and slammed the door. I rubbed my face. How could I even try to practice my routine when all I did was yell at my parents? I didn't do anything. I just sat on my bed and hugged my knees. I sat that way for a long time. Finally, there was a double knock at my door.

"Go away!" I said.

"You're supposed to answer, 'Who's there?'" Mom said softly.

"Not on your life," I shouted through the door.

"Not on your life who?" asked Mom.

She opened the door. It doesn't have a lock. I should have barricaded it.

"I'm not kidding," I said. "Go away."

"What about dinner?" she asked.

"I don't want dinner."

"You should eat before your laugh-off," said Mom. "Why don't you practice your routine on me?"

"I *can't* practice in front of you You're going to hate my routine. Most of my best jokes are about Dad, and you always take his side. How do you like this joke? 'My dad tells me that I'm so dumb that when I was little I tried to blow out lightbulbs.' Lighten up, Dad. I was just a little kid."

Mom watched me with almost no expression on her face.

"Do you want more?" I demanded. She shook her head. She left my room.

"Great," I muttered to myself. "I'm so funny, I can clear a room."

A little while later, there was a knock on my door again. "Go away, Mom," I shouted. "I don't want dinner."

"It's Dad."

"I don't want you either," I said.

Dad opened the door a crack. "Mom said that

you had some jokes about me that I should hear."

"You know," I said, "this isn't helping my confidence."

"She said it was important that I listen to your jokes," said Dad.

"Okay, Dad. Here's one from my routine: My dad doesn't like to give out compliments. He thinks that if he gives them away, he won't have any left. Come on, Dad. They're free. And think of the money you'd save. You wouldn't have to pay my friends to say nice things about me."

"I never said that," protested Dad.

"No, you just said that my friends say nice things about me, but you tell me the truth. That's a real confidence booster, Dad."

Dad chewed on his lip. I could tell he was angry, but I didn't care. "Do you want another one?"

"Yes," he said.

"If you think my dad is tough on me, you should hear what he thinks of my brother. My father is just waiting for the day that my brother gets featured on *Lifestyles of the Really Stupid*. After all, my dad's already put him on *America's Least Wanted*. My dad told both my brother and me that if we were twice as smart, we'd be half-wits. He tells us we're not complete idiots—some parts are missing."

I looked up at Dad. He wasn't laughing. "What's the matter, Dad, don't you like my jokes? How about this one: My dad's so mean that when he tried to join the human race, they turned him down."

Dad got up. "The jokes are a little cruel—especially about Jimmy." He went out and slammed my door shut.

I threw my notebook at the closed door. I bit my lip to stop myself from crying. Then I thought about watching Dad do the exact same thing. Great, like father, like son—both biting their lips in rage. I tried to take a few breaths. This was going to be wonderful. I was going to have to go onstage tomorrow, and I would probably bite my lip so hard, I'd bleed to death. Then I could shout out my last words: "Dying is easy. Comedy's hard." Some Great Laugh-Off. I don't know how long I stayed there, but finally there was a knock on my door again.

"Knock, knock," said Dad.

I didn't answer.

"It's Edwin," he said.

"Edwin who?" I asked despite myself.

"Edwin some, you lose some," said Dad. He walked in with a tray of Chinese food. "I know you're mad at me, but I really think you should eat. I told Mom and Grandma that you're too nervous to eat with us tonight—that you need to settle down and be by yourself."

I stared at the tray. He was being kind, and that was harder on me than all the times he was mean. I thought about taking back that joke about the human race.

"Thanks," I mumbled. I kept my face down. I didn't want Dad to know that I had been crying. He left the room without saying anything more.

CHAPTER 19

What do you get when you pour hot water down a rabbit hole?

A hot cross bunny!

I stayed in my room all evening. I tried to go over my routine, but the words were a blur. The phone rang about nine o'clock. "Bobby, it's for you," Mom said. I came out of my room, refusing to look her in the eye.

I picked up the phone. "One minute," said a girl's voice I didn't recognize. Then Jimmy came on the phone. "Don't say anything," he said. "I got a friend to make this call. Come on down to apartment 6A in the building. I need you. There's a poker game, and I'm losing. I told them you were my lucky charm. They think they're doing me a favor by letting me bring you."

"Uh, sorry," I said. "I can't. Tomorrow's the laugh-off."

"I need you. Please? Don't be selfish," pleaded Jimmy.

It was killing me anyway being alone in my room. I might as well ruin my chances for the laugh-off altogether. "I'll be there in a just a minute," I said into the phone. I hung up. I scratched my head. "Uh, I've got to go down to Janeen's," I said quickly to Mom, Dad and Grandma. "We've got some last-minute things to do for the laugh-off."

Dad looked at his watch. "Don't be long," he said.

"Come here," said Grandma.

"Grandma, I've got to go," I muttered. "Janeen's waiting."

"So on the way, come here," insisted Grandma. She stood up, opened her arms and drew me in. I could feel how soft she felt, as if she didn't have any bones. Her hand reached up and smooshed my hair. I was worried that I was going to cry again. What a way to spend the night before the Great Laugh-Off! I pulled away. I looked at her. "I've really got to go," I said. I could see my father and mother watching us. Grandma patted my head once more. I turned to leave.

The hallway was empty. I punched the button for the elevator. What a mess! Jimmy was waiting for me on the sixth floor. "Thanks," he said. He looked at me. "Are you okay? You look a little down in the mouth. What's the matter? Are you nervous about our signals? Let's go over them. What's the signal if someone has a straight, five cards in a row, but of different suits?"

I pretended to wipe my nose with my forefingers straight out.

Jimmy nodded. "That's good. What's the signal for a flush, five cards, all the same suit, like five hearts or five spades?"

"I say I've got to go to the toilet."

"Good. You've got a good memory, Bobby. Everything will be fine."

"Jimmy, everything is so far from fine, it isn't funny. I really do have the laugh-off tomorrow. I've got to go over my routine. Some of the jokes I was going to do—well, they're about Dad and you and me. I want to work on them. A lot of my jokes are about how mean Dad is. . . ." My voice trailed off.

"Great! I can't wait to hear them. Aren't you the one who was always telling me that comics have to make jokes about what they know? Here's a joke you can use tomorrow: Our dad is so mean, they named a cake after him—crumb!"

I shook my head. "I don't know, Jimmy. I feel . . . I can't explain it."

"Kiddo, don't worry about it. You need something to take your mind off the laugh-off. Forget about the laugh-off. Pull yourself together."

Forget about the laugh-off. The biggest thing in my life, and Jimmy wanted me to forget about it.

"Stop worrying so much," said Jimmy. "I need you on your toes."

Jimmy led me into apartment 6A. There were four people sitting around a table with an empty seat. Jimmy sat down in the empty chair. He had almost no chips in front of him. Jimmy started to deal. I recognized Mr. Young, the deli owner. He had a huge stack of poker chips in front of him. His arms were folded against his stomach, and his black hair was plastered against his skull.

"I don't like you bringing a kid," said a plump blond woman I had never seen before. She had a small stack of poker chips in front of her. Next to her was a white-haired man. His full head of white hair seemed to perch on his head like a funny cap. I couldn't tell if it was real or not. He had a substantial pile of blue chips in front of him.

"Hey, kid, make yourself useful. Bring me over a seltzer, please," he said to me. "Your brother tells us that you like jokes. Do you know what you get when you pour hot water down a rabbit hole?" he asked. I handed him his drink.

"No," I said.

"You get a hot cross bunny!" he shouted as if I were hard of hearing. I liked him. He had a big smile.

"Thank you," he said, as he took the drink. I looked at the cards in his hand. He didn't even try to hide his cards from me. Maybe he thought he was teaching me by showing me his cards. I noticed that he had five hearts in his hand. It was a flush! If Jimmy bet against him, unless he had a great hand, he would lose a lot of money.

It was Jimmy's bet. I saw him start to reach for his few remaining chips. "Uh, excuse me, I've got to go to the john," I said.

I went to the bathroom. I flushed the toilet so Jimmy would hear and remember that was our signal for a flush. I didn't want to be with these people when they found out my brother was trying to cheat them. For all the times I've gotten in trouble in school, I've never cheated. I guess Janeen really is a good influence on me in that way. I see how hard Janeen works for good grades. If I cheated, it would be like I was taking something away from her. But if I wouldn't cheat at school, why was I cheating for Jimmy? I'd always thought it was cool to help him cheat Dad when we played our family poker games, but this wasn't our family poker game.

I went back into the room. "Sorry, old guy, but a full house beats a flush any day," said Jimmy as he raked in the chips. Of course he was raking it in. I had helped him cheat.

"I was sure you were bluffing, the way you always do. I never thought you could beat a flush. Maybe I'm getting too old for this—like those darned horses I bet on."

"You're not too old," joked Jimmy. "I just got lucky. Whose deal?" Jimmy looked a little like the wolf in the pictures of "Little Red Riding Hood." He was trying to look innocent, but I had a feeling that anybody with an ounce of smarts would know that he was cheating. Maybe I had been infected by Dr. Deal's unfunny joke about a conscience being a hard thing to kill. Mine was certainly alive and kicking right now. "Uh, Jimmy," I stammered, "I can't stay. Tomorrow's a big day for me."

"What's tomorrow?" asked the old man.

"My school's having a laugh-off—a joke contest between the teachers and the kids. It was my idea."

"A joke contest in school. It sounds like a lot more fun than when I was a kid."

"Good night, everybody," I said. I went out into the hall. I ran to the elevator and pushed the button. Jimmy caught up with me. "What are you doing?" he said. He grabbed my arm.

"I've got to go home. I've got to get to bed." The elevator came. I jumped in. Jimmy came with me.

"Bobby, you're being selfish," said Jimmy. "You're leaving me just as I'm starting to win."

I felt like crying. I was so tired. "I'm not selfish. And you're not winning. You're cheating."

The elevator opened on our floor.

Jimmy followed me. He dogged me all the way to our door. "You know who's the big laugh-off?" he shouted at me. "You are. A kid who doesn't know that blood is thicker than anything else. If that teacher you love told you to jump off a bridge, would you do it?"

"You sound just like Dad," I taunted him. "And my teacher isn't you. He wouldn't ask me to jump off a bridge. Mr. Matous wouldn't ask me to do anything that would hurt me." I was shouting now. I was really angry.

"Is that a joke?" Jimmy screamed at me.

"No," I yelled, turning to face him. "It is not a joke."

I saw Jimmy's face change as if he had seen a ghost. His mouth dropped open. His lips got white.

"What's wrong?" I asked him.

I turned around. Dad was standing there. He and Jimmy stared at each other.

Dad put his arms around me. It was the strangest gesture. I don't remember him holding me like that in years. Dad looked straight at Jimmy. "What are you doing with Bobby? He's got to rest tonight. Tomorrow's his big day."

"The almighty Great Laugh-Off," said Jimmy sarcastically.

"It's important to him," said Dad. "How are you doing, Jimmy?"

"A lot you care," sneered Jimmy. "What are you doing in the hall?"

"I was looking for Bobby. I realized that he couldn't have been with Janeen. When Bobby answered the phone a little while ago, he told whoever called that he had the laugh-off tomorrow. Then he told us he was going to see Janeen, who knows as much about the Great Laugh-Off as Bobby does. I didn't want to get Mom and Grandma nervous, but I thought I'd try to find where Bobby had really gone."

Jimmy glared at him. "Congratulations, Dad. You're a great detective," he said in a mocking voice. He sounded angry and hurt. Then he looked down at me. "You know what, Bobby?" he said. "You'll lose tomorrow at that laugh-off. You know why? Because you are like everyone in this family, a born loser—a big fat loser."

"Don't speak to your brother like that," said Dad.

"Oh, so now Bobby's the fair-haired one, and I'm the monster."

"You're not a monster, Jimmy," said Dad. For a second, I thought Dad was going to cry. I had never seen Dad cry.

I saw Jimmy take a deep breath as if he'd forgotten to breathe until just now. He couldn't look at me. "I'm sorry I called you a loser, Bobby," he muttered. "Good luck tomorrow." He turned to go.

"You promised you'd come to the laugh-off," I shouted after him. I looked at Dad. "I want Jimmy there."

"Jimmy, wait," shouted Dad. Jimmy turned to face him. He still looked angry. "Go to bed, Bobby. Leave Jimmy and me alone a minute."

"Dad . . . I'm sorry," I said. I started to try to explain why I had lied about sneaking out of the apartment.

Dad shook his head. "It's not you who has to be sorry," he said. He was looking straight at Jimmy.

"Do you mean me?" Jimmy asked angrily.

Dad shook his head. "No," he said softly.

CHAPTER 20

Knock, knock.

Who's there?

Oscar.

Oscar Who?

Oscar stupid question,
you get a stupid answer.

I thought that I wouldn't be able to sleep at all,
but I was wrong. Grandma came into my room
and gently shook me. "Wake up, sleepyhead. It's
time to rise and be funny."

I rubbed my eyes. "I don't feel funny."

"You're going to knock 'em dead. You're
going straight to the top. I just want to live long
enough to see it."

I went into the bathroom and washed my face.
I thought that I would look terrible, but I surprised

myself. I looked a lot more wide-awake than I expected. My eyes were bright—like marbles.

I went out into the kitchen. Mom and Dad were both drinking coffee. There was a small rectangular package by my plate. It was tied with a big blue bow. "What's this?" I asked.

"It's from your grandmother and me," said Mom. "Grandma found it."

"But you paid for it," said Grandma to my mother.

I opened the package. It was an outrageously wide tie with a gazillion happy faces on it. It was so stupid that it was funny.

"When you look down, you'll see all those smiling faces—just like when you look out at the audience," said Mom. "Grandma pointed that out. We thought it would bring you good luck."

"It's great. But Grandma, Mom, I don't wear ties. Nobody wears ties to school."

"You'll wear one today," said Grandma. "Your father will help you tie it."

Dad looked up from his newspaper. He pretended to blink as he looked at the tie. "Nice outfit for a court jester," he said. "That tie's so loud, it needs a muffler."

"Why does everything out of your mouth have to be so mean?" said Mom. She got up and put her coffee cup in the sink. She turned and faced him. "I can't stand it when you're sarcastic to the boys. If you keep it up, we'll lose them both."

I stared at Mom. I couldn't believe she was finally standing up to Dad about his silly joke about a tie. Actually, the tie *was* so loud, it needed a muffler.

"We took a lot of time picking out that tie for Bobby," said Grandma. She glared at my father. "Go help him put it on."

"Come on, Bobby," said Dad. I couldn't believe this was all happening over a tie. I have the weirdest family in the universe. Dad put his arm on my shoulder and led me to the living-room mirror on the far side of the room. His hand felt warm. He showed me how to take the fat part of the tie under and over until I had a knot. "Now the knot should slide," said Dad, doing it for me. "Just pull. But not too hard, or you'll choke yourself."

I looked up at him. "Do you think I'll choke in the laugh-off?"

"Of course not," Dad said, maybe a little bit too quickly. He straightened my tie. "It looks great on you. I didn't mean to say that it was too loud." He glanced toward the kitchen. "I guess I never realized how my little jokes sound."

"Well, Dad, this tie isn't exactly quiet," I said. "The fashion police will probably put out an all-points bulletin for me." Suddenly, I just couldn't take not knowing anymore. "Dad, what happened with Jimmy?" I blurted out.

"I asked him to consider coming home. He said he'll think about it," said Dad.

I thought of Jimmy saying that Dad would rather be right than have him back. Now Jimmy was going to have to deal with the fact that *he* was wrong.

Dad looked down at me. "Do you think Jimmy will change?" I asked him. As soon as the words were out, I knew it was a stupid question.

Dad shrugged.

"Knock, knock," I said.

"Who's there?" asked Dad.

"Oscar."

"Oscar who?"

"Oscar stupid question, you get a stupid answer," I said.

"That's pretty funny," Dad said in a deadpan voice. I couldn't tell if he thought it was funny or not. "Except, there are no stupid questions," he added. "Particularly the one you asked about Jimmy."

Grandma yelled to us from the kitchen. "Let me see you in that tie," she shouted.

"You'd better go show her," said Dad. His voice sounded gentle. I went in and showed off my tie.

"You look so cute!" said Mom.

I frowned and grabbed my backpack. "Cute isn't exactly the look I'm going for," I said.

"You look wonderful," said Grandma. "We'll see you at the Great Laugh-Off."

"Don't worry," said Dad. "I'm prepared to laugh my head off."

I had a sudden horrible vision of Dad trying to laugh so loudly at the jokes about him that he would embarrass everybody.

"Please, Dad. Please don't laugh *too* hard at my jokes."

"I don't get it," said Dad. "I can't do anything right. If I laugh at your jokes, I'm in trouble with you. If I don't, I'm in trouble with your mom and my mom."

"Just try enjoying yourself," said Grandma. "Go on, Bobby. Don't worry about us. We'll be there. Just go out there and slaughter them."

"Mom, are you encouraging my son to be a mass murderer?" asked Dad. I knew he was kidding.

"That's comic talk," said Grandma. "I want Bobby to make them laugh so hard, the audience has to beg for mercy."

"I knew that," said Dad. He patted me on the shoulder. I kissed Mom and Grandma goodbye. As Grandma gave me a kiss, she whispered,

"Just listen to your heart."

"Grandma, what does that mean?"

"Don't worry about it," she said.

I rolled my eyes. The last thing I needed right now was to have to worry about listening to my heart—as if I didn't have enough things on my mind.

CHAPTER 21

What do you get if you cross one principal with another principal?

Don't try it— principals don't like to be crossed.

Janeen was waiting for me downstairs. She was dressed in white ribbed tights, black ankle boots, a black skirt and a white cotton sweater. The second she saw me, her face turned red and she looked down at her shoes. I started to laugh. I couldn't help myself.

Janeen blushed even more.

"What's black and white and red all over?" I asked her.

Janeen looked up and gave me a suspicious look. "A newspaper?"

"No, *you*," I said. "You look like a sun-burned penguin."

Janeen looked down at herself. "I was doing

research on comedy and Lucille Ball, from *I Love Lucy*, said that comedians should wear black and white. Do I look like a dork?"

"I'm not one to talk." I opened my jacket and showed her my tie.

"Cool tie," said Janeen. "You look good in a tie. It's cute."

I looked at her. "Too cute?" I asked worriedly.

"Naw," said Janeen. She punched me lightly on the arm. We both giggled.

When we got to school, we went directly to the auditorium to make sure that everything was set up. Mr. Matous greeted us. As soon as he saw us, he started to laugh. "Did you two plan your outfits?" he asked.

"No way!" Janeen and I said in unison.

I checked the microphones to make sure they worked. Janeen and Mr. Weinstein put up a huge computer banner that read THE GREAT LAUGH-OFF!

Dr. Deal came bustling backstage. I cringed. I couldn't tell if it was because I was nervous or if it was just a natural reaction to being around the principal. "Bobby, you look great!" said Dr. Deal enthusiastically. "You look wonderful in a tie. You should be proud of yourself. I've never seen the school so excited for an assembly. We even have members of the school board coming."

My stomach turned into a hard knot.

"You know," said Dr. Deal, rubbing her hands, "I'm actually nervous. It's strange. I speak before audiences all the time, but today I'm nervous."

"That's natural," I said. "All comics are nervous before they go on. It's what makes them good. My books say to find a quiet place and breathe deeply for a minute."

"Do you read books about this?" asked Dr. Deal.

"Yeah," I said. I didn't like the way Dr. Deal sounded shocked that I might actually read a book on my own.

"You shouldn't be surprised," said Mr. Matous, defending me. "Bobby takes comedy very seriously. That's why I gave him this assignment."

Dr. Deal looked at me as if maybe I wasn't the all-time loser she had thought I was. In fact, if I dare say it, she looked at me with a little respect.

"Well," said Dr. Deal, "I'm about to make the announcement that the children can come to the auditorium. Bobby, do you need more time?"

I felt like I could use another year to get ready, but really there wasn't anything left to do. Time was racing. All that preparation, and now the Great Laugh-Off was finally here.

"We're ready," I said.

Janeen grabbed my arm. "Bobby, do you believe it? It's really happening."

I looked down at my tie. All the little faces were frowning at me. Grandma and Mom hadn't realized that from the point of view of the guy wearing the tie, it was all frowns. I tried to put the frowns out of my mind.

"I think I may throw up," I said to Janeen. From behind the curtain, we could hear the kids file into the auditorium. Dancing elephants probably would have made less noise. Now, instead of time racing, it felt like it was crawling. I felt as if I were in a science experiment, proving that Einstein was right. Everything is relative. Speaking of relatives . . . I peeked through the curtains. I saw my parents sitting in the front row. Now I really felt sick.

Mr. Matous came up to me backstage. I felt as if my feet had grown roots into the floor. "Bobby, it's time to start," said Mr. Matous. "Are you ready?"

"Ready to throw up," I muttered.

Dr. Deal took the microphone. She sounded breathy, not at all the way she normally sounded. She made a few announcements. Then she said, "And now, I'd like to introduce the organizer of this event—Bobby Garrick."

Janeen pushed me out on the stage. The lights were so bright, I could hardly see anything. I looked down at my tie again. The little frowning faces seemed to be glowing—like aliens.

I took the microphone. It squeaked. Great beginning. "Welcome to the Great Laugh-Off," I said. Nobody laughed. Waiting for my first laugh was horrible.

I blinked. "As kids, we're always getting in trouble for laughing in class. But not today!" That got a little laugh, although I knew it wasn't very funny. I think the audience was as nervous as I was. One laugh stood out from all the others. I looked out at the audience. Jimmy was standing in the back.

I swallowed hard. I continued. "Anyhow, today you get to laugh all you want in school. Your laughter will determine the winner of our laugh-off. Teachers and students are going to tell you their best jokes. At the end, the teacher who gets the most laughs and the kid who gets the most laughs will come before you in a final laugh-off, and we'll find out who's the funniest person in this school.

"So, if you're ready to laugh, I'll introduce our first contestant. It's our one and only principal, Dr. Deal. By the way, you might want to know what you get if you cross one principal with another principal. The answer is, don't try it—principals don't like to be crossed." I had decided to deal with the eight-hundred-pound-gorilla problem by putting Dr. Deal first.

Dr. Deal took the microphone from me. "After an introduction like that, I can only say"—she paused—"Bobby, wait until I get you alone."

I swallowed hard. Was I really in trouble? I thought the joke about crossing one principal with another was funny. I quickly walked offstage.

"I'm kidding," said Dr. Deal, looking offstage at where I was standing in the wings. She actually smiled at me. "I think it's wonderful what Bobby Garrick has done. But seriously folks, I'm the principal of the school," she announced. "At least, whenever my secretary allows me to be."

There were a few titters from the audience. It sounded as if nobody was sure that it was a joke.

I was drenched in sweat. I listened to Dr. Deal continue. "A vicious dog snapped at me in the street this morning. I stood in front of him and shouted, 'GO!' The dog ran away. 'Are you an animal trainer?' somebody asked me. 'No, I'm a principal,' I said."

Dr. Deal got a small laugh. She paused and looked out at the audience. "I can see that I've got an audience here who doesn't mind detention." There were a few nervous giggles. Nobody was really sure she was kidding. "Thank you all very much," said Dr. Deal.

At least she knew enough to get off the stage. She was breathing hard. She stared at me. "Bobby, you were great doing your introduction. You got more laughs than I did, and I thought my jokes were good." She looked angry, as if maybe she wanted to vaporize me for getting more laughs than she did. Was I going to get in trouble for being funnier than the principal? What had I let myself in for?

Dr. Deal took a deep breath. She seemed to pull herself together. I thought she was reminding herself that she was the person in charge, and I knew she liked being in charge. "Maybe comedy isn't my thing," she said. "I'm going to sit in the audience now. Good luck."

The "Good luck" surprised me.

☺

CHAPTER 22

What is big and green and has a trunk?
An unripe elephant.

The laugh-off was going by so quickly, I could hardly keep up with my introductions. I had to keep my clipboard with the list of contestants with me at all times.

Willie got a big laugh with really silly jokes. There was just something funny about the way he told them. "What did one eye say to the other eye?" He grinned. "Just between you and me, something smells!" He held his nose. As I said, it's a dumb joke, but it just cracked the audience up.

His second joke was even sillier. "What can a rhino do that no other animal can?" Willie paused as if the answer were going to be brilliant. "Have a baby rhino!" he shouted out. Then he doubled over with laughter as if he had just told the funniest joke in the world. He got another big laugh.

Zach, the little second-grader who had burst

into tears at rehearsal, got a great laugh with a brand-new joke. "Why did the bubblegum cross the road?" Zach asked. "It was stuck to the chicken's foot!" he shouted out in a really loud voice. He looked so happy up there. I could tell everybody just *wanted* to laugh with him. I gave him a high five as he came off. I thought he had a good chance of being the finalist kid.

Mr. Weinstein told a bunch of computer jokes. "Did you hear the one abut the lady who had a young son named Hans? He would always play with her computer after he had eaten something. He would get peanut butter and jelly and all kinds of sticky things on the keyboard. After a while, the computer couldn't stand the mess. One day, the lady turned on the computer, and this message was on the screen: 'I won't do any work for you until you take your dirty Hans off me!'"

That joke got only a middling response. The audience seemed to have gotten tired of laughing.

Tyrone had some funny jokes, but he ruined them by talking too fast. He asked, "What teaches school, is green and is wet all the time? The Teacher from the Black Lagoon." Tyrone snickered, but he said the punch line so quickly that nobody could really hear it.

"Why is it easy to fool vampires?" Tyrone asked, for his second joke. "Because they're known to be suckers," he answered, but again he said it too fast, and half the audience didn't hear him.

I looked at my list of contestants. Janeen was coming up. She had been listening to Tyrone. "This joke telling is harder than it looks, isn't it?" she said.

I nodded.

"I think I am going to vomit," she said.

"That's good," I said. "Like I told Dr. Deal, all my books on comedy say that every successful comic feels afraid. The trick is to go on even though you are still feeling afraid. The fear is supposed to go away as soon as you step onstage."

"What if it doesn't?"

"You're about to find out," I warned her. "I've got to go out and introduce you. Good luck!" I went onstage. "And now, ladies and gentlemen, boys and girls—what has two hands but can't clap?"

"I don't know," shouted a voice.

"A clock! But you're not tick-tocks, so put *your* hands together and give a big round of applause for Janeen Wilson!"

Janeen looked at me as if I were sending her to the guillotine. She seemed mad that I had told the clock joke, but I just wanted the audience to clap for her. She took the stage. She stood about a foot away from the microphone.

"What is big and green and has a trunk?"

"What?" shouted a kid from the audience who couldn't hear her.

"An unripe elephant," whispered Janeen.

"What?" shouted the kid again.

"I already told you," said Janeen. She coughed nervously. I could tell how desperate she felt, and I wished that I could help her. A comic desperate for laughs isn't a pretty sight.

"What's Smokey Bear's middle name?" asked Janeen in a whispery voice.

"What?" shouted the same kid from the audience again.

"Th-the . . ." Janeen stammered. She fled the stage. She just bolted away from the microphone and practically ran me over.

I grabbed her. The audience applauded. I couldn't tell if they were clapping because they were glad she got off the stage or because they were feeling sorry for her. "I was awful," she wailed.

"It's okay. My books say that you can learn from bombing."

"Will you stop quoting to me from your darned books?" she growled. "The only thing I've learned is that I don't ever, *ever* want to do this again."

"You're not mad at me, are you?"

"Let me go, will you?" Janeen looked furious. I let her go. The Great Laugh-Off was turning out just peachy. The principal had looked like she wanted to vaporize me, and now my best friend wanted to kill me.

CHAPTER 23

Why don't cannibals eat class clowns?
Because they taste funny.

Mr. Matous was standing in the corner with his eyes closed. I went up to him. "What are you doing?" I asked. "You're on in just a minute."

He took a few deep breaths. "I'm taking your advice."

"Mine?"

Mr. Matous nodded. "I heard you tell Dr. Deal it was a good thing to do some breathing exercises before you go on. If I can't get bigger laughs than some of the other teachers, I'll never be able to hold my head up in the teachers' lounge. I've got a lot riding on this."

"I never knew that teachers were so competitive," I said.

"Believe it," said Mr. Matous. He wiped his hands on his pants.

I left him alone. I went back onstage and took

the microphone. "I know you're going to find our next contestant funny. In his last appearance doing comedy, he drew a line three blocks long. Then they took his chalk away. And I'm not just trying to butter him up—because you all know why the cannibal got expelled from school—for buttering up his teacher. Here's my very own homeroom teacher, Mr. Matous."

"Thank you, Bobby," said Mr. Matous. He took the microphone in his hand and held it close to his mouth. Somehow he just looked very relaxed on the stage. The other teachers had looked so much more nervous. He looked over at me. "Bobby, at least you don't have to be wary of cannibals. You know why cannibals don't eat class clowns, don't you? They taste funny."

He paused and looked out at the audience. He was good! I hadn't told him that I was going to tell the cannibal joke, so his comeback was ad-libbed. I was really impressed.

"Most of you know I'm a new teacher," continued Mr. Matous. He paused again. Something about his pause made everybody laugh.

"I've learned a lot in my first year. For example, I used to think that I knew what it meant to be insane. Now I see that insanity is just part of the job description." I listened to him. He wasn't telling jokes. Mr. Matous was just making fun of himself as a new teacher, and he was getting the most laughs of any teacher.

"Being a teacher means constantly playing straight man for your kids. For example, during geography, I made the mistake of asking the class where the English Channel is located. 'We don't get that channel on our TV,' said Willie. Thanks, Willie! Then there was the time we were studying Columbus and I asked if they knew how Columbus's men slept on their ships. 'With their eyes shut,' said Sahira. I had to admit that she had the right answer.

"See, first-year teachers make a lot of mistakes. There was the day that I warned my class that we would have a test, rain or shine! They got out of it. It was snowing. Although I'm not actually sure that they didn't get Bobby Garrick to go up on the roof and sprinkle Ivory Flakes past my window."

Mr. Matous got a pretty big laugh with that one. "Don't laugh," said Mr. Matous. "You don't have Bobby in your class. There was the time that I tried to control my class. I yelled, 'Order! Children, order!' Bobby Garrick yelled out, 'A cheeseburger with fries and a Coke!' And now thanks to Bobby, we're all out here laughing. Thank you all very much."

Mr. Matous got a big round of applause. He

put the microphone back on its stand and came offstage grinning. He knew he had done well. He clapped me on the shoulder. "I hope you don't mind those stories about you—I knew it would get a big laugh."

"It's okay," I said. It surprised me how much he had remembered. Mr. Matous had sounded so natural. You could tell the difference between him and the others. He was himself. All my books said comedy wasn't about telling jokes. Jokes are easy; comedy is hard.

I went and stood in a corner. I closed my eyes. I was on soon. I tried to be calm, but my heart was beating triple fast. Grandma had told me to listen to my heart. My heart seemed to be telling me to run away. I swallowed hard. My brain shut down completely. I couldn't remember any of my act.

I left my corner and stood just offstage. Mr. Matous had agreed to introduce me. He bounded back onto the stage. Somehow his energy seemed a little too much for me. Suddenly I realized why Dr. Deal and Janeen had sounded so annoyed when I got big laughs for introducing them. "Okay, boys and girls. Our next contestant is Bobby Garrick. Once I made the mistake of asking Bobby Garrick to name one important thing that we have today that we didn't have ten years ago. 'ME!' said Bobby. And he's absolutely right. Without him, none of us would be enjoying ourselves this morning. So let's put our hands together for the boy who gave us this Great Laugh-Off. Here's Bobby!"

I walked onstage feeling as dead on my feet as a zombie. I looked at the microphone in front of me. When I had gone on to introduce the others, I'd had no trouble grabbing the microphone and holding it close, but now I felt as if one part of my brain were shouting, "That thing can electrocute you—don't go near it. Mayday! Bail out!"

I made myself take a deep breath. I lowered the microphone and put it close to my mouth. My mouth felt so dry, I wasn't sure that I could speak.

"Hi," I said.

I got a few hi's back, but everybody seemed to be waiting for me to say something. They all thought I was going to be hilarious. "Thanks, Mr. Matous," I said. There was a pause. People were waiting for me to make a joke back at Mr. Matous, but my mind was literally a blank. I couldn't believe it. I had read about it happening. I froze. I was bombing even before I opened my mouth.

I scratched my head. "Head lice," I muttered into the microphone. There were a few laughs. I could recognize Grandma's laugh. I relaxed a little bit. I remembered what I had practiced with Grandma.

"I've always wanted a pet—but our apartment is too small." I took the microphone off the stand and walked toward the audience. Out of the corner of my eye I could see Mom and Dad, sitting in the front row to the side. Mom kept twisting her neck around, trying to see if Jimmy was still there.

I didn't want to think about my family. I searched the audience to find Janeen's face in the audience, but everything was a blur. I could see little Zach looking up to me. I knew he was pulling for me. I pretended to talk directly to him. "I finally got a pet small enough to keep in my apartment. Head lice. You can pick them up at school anytime. I've taught mine how to do tricks."

I could see people starting to scratch their heads. "Go ahead—scratch," I ad-libbed. I got a big laugh.

I paused to let it sink in. I remembered how well Mr. Matous's pauses worked, and my comedy books all said that you had to give the audience time to react—time to laugh.

I looked out at Grandma. I grinned at her. "I love my funky head lice. We get these notes from school. No child will be admitted with head lice.

Is that fair? Isn't that discrimination? Someday, one of the little head lice dancing in my hair is going to rise up and say, 'Why can't we all just get along?' Head lice and children sitting in classrooms peacefully together—it could be so beautiful.

I paused for a second. "But seriously, there's a lot we could learn from head lice—like how to do the jitterbug. And just think, we could teach them knock-knock jokes."

That got a big laugh from the audience. I could even see my father laughing. I thought about the time he said that I should outgrow knock-knock jokes. "I bet I can guess what their first one will be. Knock, knock," I shouted out.

"Who's there?" yelled the kids in the audience.

"Police," I yelled.

"Police who?" shouted back Jimmy, so loudly that his voice floated over everybody's. It was one of his favorite jokes. Mom twisted in her seat again. Grandma looked back at Jimmy.

"Po-*lice* stop telling me these stupid knock-knock jokes," I said. I paused again. "My brother taught me that joke," I said. I grinned at him. "He's here today, and he taught me lots of jokes."

I licked my lips. I thought of all the jokes I had written about how dumb my father thought Jimmy was. I couldn't say them. I felt as if my brain were splitting in front of me. I needed to go with a safe joke. I remembered one about a parrot that I had heard on TV. "As I said, we can't have pets in our apartment building, so I hang out in pet stores. I saw a parrot for sale. He had a red ribbon tied on one foot and a blue ribbon tied on the other.

"'What are the ribbons for?' I asked the pet store owner. 'It's a very special parrot,' said the owner. 'It was trained to talk by pulling on its ribbons. If you pull the red ribbon, the parrot will sing the "Star-Spangled Banner." If you pull the blue ribbon, the parrot will recite the Gettysburg Address.' 'What happens if I pull both ribbons at the same time?' I asked. And the parrot screeched, 'I'll fall off my perch, stupid!'"

That got a big laugh. I paused to appreciate the sound of it. I was sweating so much, I thought I was having meltdown. All my books on comedy said to get off the stage when you got a big laugh. I put my mouth as close to the microphone as I could. "Thank you," I said.

I ran off the stage. I was shaking all over. I ran to the bathroom backstage by the band room. I could taste vomit in my mouth. It was all too much. Jimmy, Mom, Dad, Grandma—the jokes— the pressure of being onstage. The fact that I had lost my nerve. I hadn't even told any of my best jokes. I threw up. Luckily, I missed my tie.

CHAPTER 24

What do you get when you cross
a werewolf with a dozen eggs?

A hairy omelet.

I splashed water on my face. I heard a knock on the bathroom door. "Go away," I said.

"Knock, knock." I recognized Janeen's voice.

"I said go away."

"Knock, knock," repeated Janeen.

"I'm not going to say 'who's there'!" I yelled through the bathroom door.

"Arthur."

"Arthur who?" I asked despite myself.

"Arthur any kids in there who can come out?" asked Janeen.

I took a deep breath. I opened the bathroom door. Janeen was the one person I couldn't lock out. "I was sick to my stomach."

"I heard," said Janeen.

"I forgot almost my whole routine," I lied. I

hadn't forgotten it. I just didn't have the guts to go through with it.

"Bobby, nobody cared," said Janeen. "While you were being sick in the bathroom, you won the kids' part of the Great Laugh-Off! Now it's between you and Mr. Matous. It couldn't be better. The funniest teacher against the funniest kid. It's perfect."

"I don't think I can go on," I said.

"You told me that all comics have to conquer fear and go on even if they're afraid. Now you're going to wimp out? No way!"

"This is different, Janeen," I said.

Mr. Matous came up to us. He held out his hand to me. "Congratulations," he said. "It's you against me. Are you ready?"

I started to shake. Literally. My right leg had a nerve in it that was out of control. I tried to stop it, but I couldn't. "See? Even my leg is shaking. It's telling me not to go on. I'm sorry, Mr. Matous. I don't have any more jokes."

"What about all those jokes you said you forgot?" argued Janeen.

"What's the problem?" asked Dr. Deal, coming backstage. "The audience is stamping its feet. We have to start the final laugh-off soon."

"Bobby needs a few seconds to pull himself together," said Mr. Matous. "I'll go on first."

I looked up in horror. Mr. Matous followed my gaze. Mom and Dad had burst into the back-stage area. Right behind them were Jimmy and Grandma. Grandma was looking proud and happy. But I wouldn't say the same for my parents. Mom looked nervous and twitchy, and Dad just looked nervous.

"Is anything wrong?" asked Mom anxiously. "They announced that Bobby was going to be in the final laugh-off, but there seemed to be a long delay."

"Is Bobby in trouble?" Dad asked Dr. Deal.

Mr. Matous didn't give Dr. Deal the time to answer. "Didn't you hear the laughter out there?" Mr. Matous said. He sounded angry. "Bobby won. He won because of the hard and intelligent work he did."

"Bobby," said my father, "I've always said you're a kid of rare intelligence. It's just rare when you show any."

"Can't you ever stop!" Mom hissed at him.

"Very funny, Dad," said Jimmy. "I'm sure Bobby appreciated that—especially at a time like this."

Dad's eyes widened. "It was just a little joke," he said quietly, using his all-purpose excuse. Dad seemed to wait for Dr. Deal and Mr. Matous to take his side. They didn't. He looked so uncomfortable, I almost felt sorry for him.

"I think that Bobby's one of the most creative students I'll ever have," said Mr. Matous. "It's been a privilege to teach him."

"Mr. Garrick," said Dr. Deal, "I too have been very impressed with the work Bobby did to pull this assembly together."

"Why don't you tell them that they're both very impressionable, Dad," I muttered.

Dad wouldn't look at me. I could feel the lousy taste from the throw-up in my mouth. "Mr. Matous, you won," I said. "I don't have any more jokes."

"If you quit now, you'll never know how good you could be," said Mr. Matous.

I glared at him. "I won't go on. You can't make me."

"You're right," said Mr. Matous. "I can't make you. But if you do go on, I hope to beat the pants off you. May the best comic win." He walked away, leaving me alone with my family. Talk about not-funny situations. Just what I needed— my family!

Dad looked at Grandma and then at Mom and Jimmy. "Uh, Bobby, can I speak to you for a minute alone?" he asked. Dad took me over to a corner where all the instruments for the band were kept. He stood beside the big kettledrum.

"When I made that crack about you being a kid of rare intelligence," he said, "it just slipped out. I didn't mean it."

"Right," I said sarcastically. I was exhausted. I thought about all the times I had sounded just like him—telling Janeen that my put-downs had just slipped out.

"You can't quit," Dad said.

"Everybody's telling me that," I snapped. "But it's not true. I can. If I want to quit, nobody can stop me. Even Mr. Matous, and he likes me a lot more than you do."

Dad looked as if he had been slapped. "I love you," he protested.

"Maybe," I mumbled. "But you don't like me—not the way Mr. Matous and Janeen do."

"You don't really think that, do you?" He looked really hurt.

I didn't say anything.

"Don't drop out just to spite me. You're too funny to let yourself down like this."

"Too funny for my own good. Isn't that what you always say? You heard some of my routine. Do you really want to hear those things in public? All those jokes about how mean you are—how you're always telling Jimmy and me that we're dumb? Those are my funniest jokes."

Dad shook his head. "You're wrong. Those

aren't your funniest jokes. That's not why Mr. Matous and Janeen like you so much. I don't mind you making fun of me, but don't . . ." He paused.

"Don't what exactly, O Wise One?" I demanded.

"Don't be sarcastic, Bobby. Don't use jokes to hurt people."

"Well, I learned from the expert," I said.

Dad didn't say anything. He just looked down at his shoes. I had finally stumped him—he didn't have a comeback for that. So why didn't I feel good about it? "I'm sorry," I started to say, but Dad interrupted me.

"You know what's so ironic?" he asked me.

I shook my head. I half expected him to ask me if I knew the meaning of "ironic," but he didn't.

"I always wanted to make my own father laugh. But my dad always reacted to my humor as though I had really laid an egg."

I looked up at him. "You should have asked Grandpa what happens if you cross a werewolf with a dozen eggs."

"What happens?" asked Dad.

"You get a hairy omelet," I answered.

Dad laughed. It was a dry laugh, as if he didn't really have any air in his lungs. "Bobby, you really

... for every occasion."

... eld me by the shoulders and looked at
... i love you, kiddo. Now get out there and
...ay them—or whatever the saying is."

"It's 'slaughter them,' Dad."

Dad straightened my tie. "I want you to win
the Great Laugh-Off," he said.

"I'm not doing this just for you," I warned
him.

"I know," said Dad.

I took a deep breath. "Okay," I said.

Dad gave me a quick hug. "I'm so very, very,
sorry, son," he whispered.

I stared at him. Dad had said, "I'm sorry." He
had even said, "I'm very, very sorry." They were
the last words I ever expected to hear from him.

It was time for my final routine, and I wasn't
sure that my best jokes worked anymore. I was a
comic in big, big trouble.

☺

CHAPTER 25

What's too funny for our own good?

I listened to the end of Mr. Matous's routine. He was pretty funny, but most of his jokes were kind of the same as his first set. "The kids in my class need a little help with their grammar," he said. "Sometimes I give them examples of improper English and ask them to correct it. I wrote on the board, 'I didn't have no fun at the seashore' and asked, 'How should I fix this?' 'Get a date,' shouted Bobby Garrick." It had happened way in the beginning of the year. I had completely forgotten about it.

I stopped listening to him. I had to think about my own routine. Everything felt so mixed up. Jokes were easier for me when I knew exactly how I felt about everybody. Grandma was nice; Dad was mean; Mom was scared of her own shadow, and my brother was a screwup. How was I supposed to win the Great Laugh-Off if nobody stayed the same? Who was I supposed to make fun of? I knew the answer: Me.

I heard Mr. Matous say, "Thank you all very much."

Mr. Matous came offstage. He looked like he had just swum the English Channel all by himself. "Okay, Bobby, it's your turn. Just remember, right now there's no such thing as being too funny."

I took the stage. My heart was pounding. I felt totally out of control. I forced myself to breathe as I looked out across the bright lights. I took the microphone, and my hands were so sweaty, the microphone flew into the air. I juggled it. There was a titter of nervous laughter. I was dying inside. I could feel the audience staring at me. They weren't sure whether to laugh or not. The entire audience grew silent. I was drenched in sweat. I was bombing right in front of their eyes. I could see Dad in the audience. He looked so nervous.

I scratched my head. "The head lice in my hair are coming out to rescue me any minute," I said. "Those little buggers never forget a joke."

The audience laughed loudly. They were with me again. They had remembered the joke from my first routine. I had done a callback. Now I had a choice. I could keep going making safe jokes about bugs, or I could go for the jugular. All great comics have to go for the jugular.

"My dad has this habit," I said. There was a pause. I could tell people were on edge. What was I going to say? Was I going to reveal something really embarrassing about Dad—something that nobody wanted to hear?

"He loves to ask questions that you should never answer. All adults do this, but my dad is a perfectionist about it. A perfectionist is someone who takes infinite pains to get something right— but in my dad's case it means he gives everyone around him infinite pains in the butt . . . specially my mom, me and my brother."

I could hear Jimmy laughing harder than anybody. A lot of the kids and teachers knew about Jimmy and me always getting into trouble, but even the ones who didn't were laughing. The kids were catching on that it was okay to laugh at your parents and your family today.

I looked out at the audience, and Dad was looking up at me. "My dad is always asking me, 'Where are you manners?'" I paused. The audience laughed—but a little anxiously. "Does he think I know where my manners are?" I blurted out. "Gee, Dad, they were here a few minutes ago, but they've gone to Disney World. They'll send you a postcard. It'll be a very, very polite postcard. 'Dear Bobby's parents, Thank you for the lovely stay at your house with Bobby. But we won the Superbowl of Manners, and we got to go to Disney World. Wish you were here!'"

I got a laugh with that one. It just came rolling in on me—a gigantic wave of sound. I fiddled with the microphone. I thought the audience would get restless, but they seemed willing to wait for me. I swallowed and tried not to look at Dad, but it was hard. My eyes kept going back to him.

"Here's another question that my dad likes to ask: 'How many times do I have to tell you this?' Keep going, Dad, you're near the record."

"You know, Dad also seems to have an obsession with the idea that my friends are all going to jump off a bridge. 'If the other kids all jumped off a bridge, would you jump?' It's one of his favorite questions. How can I answer that? Oh yeah, Dad. I just came home to get my bathing suit."

The laughs were pouring in now. All the kids who had to listen to their parents ask them these dumb questions were howling their heads off.

I nodded and grinned. "I mean, where do parents *get* these questions? Do they get an instructional manual when we're born? Here, ask these questions, and you'll drive your kids crazy."

I looked out again. Dad and Grandma were both cracking up. Even Mom had a real smile on her.

I was making fun of Dad, but not of myself. I

looked out at the audience. "Changing is hard," I blurted out. "Doing it up here onstage—it's like trying to suck a dinosaur up your nose." I knew the audience didn't exactly know what I meant, but they were with me. They would follow me anywhere. I took a deep breath. I was flying without a net.

"See, I should tell the truth. I was born with an instruction manual on how to drive my parents and all adults crazy. Just before I was delivered, a little voice whispered into my ear—'Bobby, be a joker.'

"I think kids and adults are programmed to drive each other nuts. Kids are born just knowing that someday we'll get to yell at our parents, 'How come you're so mean?' If that doesn't get them, I always try, 'Don't you remember what it's like to be a little kid?' Well, guess what I just found out? My dad does remember what it's like to be a kid. He wishes he could forget—but he can't. I guess the good parents can't forget."

My dad had a funny look on his face.

"See, Dad," I shouted out. "There's really no such thing as being too funny!"

"You're right!" my dad shouted back.

There was a silence from the audience. Dad's answer had broken my comic routine. But I knew what Dad was trying to tell me. He was telling me that no matter what happened with the Great Laugh-Off, we had both won a much bigger contest.

I scratched my head. "Gee, Dad," I said. "You even got my head lice jumping with that one. Now I'm sorry I put some of these little buggers on your pillow last night." I shrugged and looked sheepishly out at the audience. "Just kidding!" Dad was laughing so hard, tears were running down his face.

I was nearly done. I looked out at the audience. I played it straight. "Now, I've got one last question for you—What's too funny for our own good? I think the answer is: nothing. Nothing is *too* funny, and there's enough funny stuff for all of us."

I took a bow. Sweat was running down my armpits and my back. I almost couldn't breathe. I gulped. I felt like my insides were melting away. I wiped my eyes. I hadn't been funny. I was sure I had been too serious, but kids were stamping their feet and cheering! Maybe they were just glad that I had finally left the stage.

Ms. Lofti came out onstage with Mr. Matous and Dr. Deal. "Girls and boys," said Ms. Lofti. "As the official laugh-a-meter for the Great Laugh-Off, I declare that the final laugh-off has been won—by Bobby Garrick. Let's give him a big round of applause. Bobby, you've won a month's supply of pizza, and this trophy!"

I stared at the trophy. Mr. Matous handed it to me. It was a giant gold cup, the kind you see locked up in cases in the hallway at school—that's how big it was. I looked inside, and sitting in there was a giant jar of Vaseline. I started to laugh. "I got it in case you won," Mr. Matous whispered.

I took the Vaseline out and waved in the air. "A joker's best friend!" I shouted. My class cracked up.

I saw Grandma and Mom and Dad standing up in the first row.

I took the microphone. "Thank you, everybody," I said. "I want to thank my grandmother, who has always laughed at my jokes; my brother, who taught me my first knock-knock joke; and my mom, who's responsible for this tie." I waved its ends in the air. The audience laughed, and Mom looked pleased.

"But most of all, I want to really thank my dad. Once I got mad at him when he said that I got my sense of humor from him. But now I've got to say thank you, Dad. I think I did."

Then I did something that I never thought I would do. I jumped off the stage. I went to where my dad was sitting. I took his hand. He shook his head, but I tugged at him, and brought him up onstage. Later Janeen said she wanted me up on the stage all by myself, but see, I know something. I'm going to get plenty of chances to be up there by myself—but this was a time I wanted Dad up there with me—to let him know that I loved him and that he was funny too.